# LONDON

# Sharp and Short

# Six Stories Featuring DI Harry Hawkins

Garry and Roy Robson

# London Large: Sharp and Short

Published by London Large Publishing

ISBN -Book            978-0-9934338-6-3

ISBN – Paperback -    978-1-9993153-2-0

For more copies of this book, please email: info@londonlarge.com

Cover Designed by Spiffing Covers: http://spiffingcovers.com/

# TABLE OF CONTENTS

# Home Front

# November 2003 – 3am

Some days he wished he'd never left the army. There was too much weight on his shoulders now; too much to think about, to get through, to be in charge of. Too much of the world's sickness to chase down and confront; too much time wrestling with the knot in his stomach, trying to prevent it from strangling the whole of him; too much, when it came to it, of the world, and of himself.

He couldn't get out of the car. The rain, hammering down in vertical sheets, looked as black as the road, the buildings, the dirt on the construction sites and the corrugated iron fencing around them – as black as the whole sickening nocturnal landscape of the nether end of King's Cross.

Was he still drunk, or just hungover? Was he just tired and fed up, or depressed? Was he half-asleep, or half-awake? Was this reality, or a nightmare he was trying to shake off? He couldn't get out of the car – not in this weather, not at this time of night, not in this man-made desolation. Not to look at the violated body of yet another young girl, photographed, catalogued, picked over and assessed by people looking as exhausted and sick at heart as he felt.

He thought of Grace, his little Grace, tucked up and snoring sweetly in her bed at home. Four years old, without a care in the world. For now. But she had it coming, he knew – she had it coming. The wrenching in his gut tightened, and sent a wave of intense choking despair up into his chest, his throat, his eyes.

How old would the girl he would have to look at soon be? The last one was seventeen, the one before nineteen, the one before that – the first – fifteen. All found in their pitiful resting places in or near the rougher, more desperate red-light districts, all on the run from only God knew what in the North or Scotland.

It was almost three o'clock. If he left it any longer he wouldn't make it. He'd fall asleep and need to ask his DS, Budgie McAllister, to just do everything and cover for him. But he'd never asked anyone to cover for him in his life, for anything; if he started now he'd be on a slippery slope. He took a double-slug from his flask, threw open the door like he hated it and surged as best he could towards the piece of waste ground where all the flashing lights were, where she would be.

No one demanded to see any ID. He'd been the most famous copper in London for over a decade now, but his heading-up of the murders of these girls had made him familiar to the whole country. Harry Hawkins had gone national.

H knew his way around the darkness of the world: the horror of war, the vile bestiality of human nature at its worst, the remorseless grind of evil and suffering that it was his lot to try and contain. In doing his duty he was as brave as a lion and as solid as a rock; everybody knew that. What they couldn't know was that the lion was losing heart, the rock was crumbling from the inside and that the prospect of the sight of another mutilated girl now filled him with terror. Sooner or later, he felt, something was going to tip him over the edge – and the pitiless snuffing out of young female life was the most likely candidate, the thing he hated most about the world, and about living in it.

He ducked under the tape around the crime scene and found Budgie McAllister on the job. He was crouched down close by the body, peering into the heart of darkness.

'Alright Budge, what we looking at son?'

'More of the same, skipper. More of the fucking same,' said Budgie. He'd worked hard to take the edge off his Glasgow accent, so that people down south could understand him. A couple of years at the University of Glasgow studying for a Masters in criminology had helped.

But he still had the swagger and bounce and terrier-like intensity of the street about him, and this gave him a personality profile much appreciated by H: he had brains and balls, unlike so many in his cohort, who tended to have a bit of either one or the other. Budgie McAllister had both.

H rode the wave of nausea that swept over him for a few seconds. 'So, another one to add to the list, as far as you can tell?' he said.

'Yes, I would say so skipper. Look for yourself,' said Budgie, drawing the plastic sheet further down from the girl's face, revealing her chest.

H was now glad of the rain – it was falling so hard it was difficult to see anything much, and difficult even to speak. He threw a quick glance in the direction of the body, but registered little. He signalled to Budgie to pull the sheet back up, and approached him as he stood back up, putting his arm firmly around his shoulders.

'Listen Budge, I'm not feeling all that clever. Can you hold the fort here for me? I've got an appointment at the hospital at nine o'clock. St Thomas'. I could do with a little rest beforehand. Just a little procedure, won't take long. I'll be back in the office before lunchtime.'

'Course I can skipper, no problem. Nothing serious I hope?'

'Nah, nothing serious. Just a little test.'

# 9am

They were running late. H flicked once again through the collection of women's and home and garden magazines in the waiting area, looking for something to engage his interest – why was it never football or boxing stuff, something like that, he wondered? – and looked at his watch.

He hated hospitals. They always put him in mind of inactivity, passivity, helplessness…and recently he'd had to spend a lot of time in them with his father. He'd had a bellyful of them, and now here he was, trapped inside one on his own account.

A door opened, disgorging a bulky but vigorous looking older man in green working pyjamas and white clogs. 'Mr. Hawkins?' he enquired. 'Yep, me – that's me,' said H.

He was ushered into a room with a padded bench at the centre, surrounded by a bank of machines, and asked to sit down.

'So, I'd just like to ask you a few questions, Mr. Hawkins, before we get started. First, what makes you think you need to have a colonoscopy?' said the doctor.

'Well, I'm forty-five now and my doctor told me a while ago that it was about time I started having them. Then my old man got liver cancer…'

'Did he survive it?'

'Yep, they said he was in the clear at his last check-up.'

'That's exceptional.'

'Yeah, well, he's hard as nails.'

'And you, Mr. Hawkins? Are you well? Any major illnesses or conditions I should know about?'

'You've got my medical records there in front of you, haven't you?'

'Yes, but I'm asking you…Are you hard as nails as well?'

'Yep. No health problems that I know of. I've had a touch of PTSD from my army days, but physically I'm as fit as a butcher's dog. Always have been.'

'So, you exercise? Eat well?'

'Well, I'm a policeman. I'm very active physically – you have to be, chasing villains and murderers up and down. And my wife keeps me well-fed.'

'I thought you chaps just sat behind computers these days?'

'Some of them do. Not me.'

'Smoke?'

'No.'

'Drink?'

'Yep, all the time. Scotch, mostly. You could probably classify me as a functioning alcoholic if you felt like it.'

'You weren't drinking yesterday I hope?'

'Nah, I was purging, as instructed. Didn't touch a drop.'

\*\*\*

It wasn't until he was up on the bench that he realized how scared he was. He'd never had any serious physical health problems, but the glimpse of mortality he'd got through his father's ordeal had shaken him more than he'd admitted to himself. He'd seen plenty people killed, and the wrecked bodies of countless murder victims, and he'd dispatched his fair share of bad guys himself, but he'd never really connected these things to his own eventual demise.

The probe went in painlessly enough. But it was what happened next that shocked him – the sight of his insides on the screen, his own mysterious, hidden-away blood and guts. *Why do they always assume you want to watch all this stuff these days?* he thought. He didn't want to, but he couldn't help himself, so he focused on the screen and grimaced, appalled and waiting for the worst, at the endless barrelling down through passages, chambers, tunnels, spirals. The probe pumped air and squirted water continually to clear the bile, which was everywhere, out of the way of the lens. On and on it went, down and down, with H watching through narrowed eyes and gritted teeth as at a horror film, waiting for the monster to rear up around the next bend. But it didn't; there was nothing, not so much as a little polyp. It was all as clean as a whistle – after everything he'd thrown at it.

*Fuck me, I've got away with it...unbelievable.*

'Well,' said the doctor to H, dressed again and back in the chair, 'that's all very satisfactory, I must say, for a man of your habits. All clear. I'd get your liver checked out if I were you though. But as far as I'm concerned, see you in ten years.'

H walked out of the hospital in reflective mood. He'd had a result, there was no doubt about that. A new lease of life, sort of. But now he would have to return to life, to the world, to his problems. He'd been granted a clean bill of health, and now he'd have to use it to wade through the quagmire that he felt himself being sucked into, deeper and deeper every day.

It was still raining. He walked across Westminster Bridge anyway, veered over towards Westminster Central Hall, along Storey's Gate and into the Westminster Arms, where he sunk in quick succession three pints of bitter with whiskey chasers.

Now he was ready to face the day. He walked across, through the rain, to New Scotland Yard.

11

# 12pm

He arrived at the press conference in belligerent mood, more than ready to treat the assembled hacks and their audiences to the kind of cantankerous, attritional performance he was becoming famous for. He hated the spotlight and the media, but they loved him: he made for great TV and radio, and the banner headlines in the tabloids, spun around his bloody-minded candour and old-school aphorisms, did nothing to hurt sales.

But it was his bear-like, no-nonsense demeanour that spoke loudest. People either loved him, he was learning, or hated him. There was not much in between. Now, facing the massed ranks of one of the world's most cynical and intrusive medias, he found himself in a strange mood: the results of the colonoscopy and the drinks he'd had to celebrate them had put him in a better mood than he'd been used to lately; they had lifted his spirits sufficiently to relish the prospect of the confrontation.

H was ready to go.

He looked out into the sea of hack faces, popping flashbulbs and TV cameras and steadied his resolve – he knew that he would soon be facing the usual barrage of ill-informed, clichéd and unanswerable questions and attacks on his competence, and he was ready to give as good as he got. Chief Superintendent Alistair Newcombe, who loved H's murder clear-up rate and accepted that he had his own way of doing things, asking only that he curb his swearing in public settings, opened proceedings. He introduced H, gave a short summary of what was known about the previous evening's murder, and invited questions.

All of these, as usual, were directed at H. First up was Bob Pritchard of *The Sun*, one of the best-known of the tabloid world's grizzled crime reporters.

12

'DI Hawkins, are you connecting last night's murder to the others you have been investigating lately? Are you working on the assumption that it may be the work of The Crawler?'

'I don't make assumptions, Bob. I go by facts. Small, solid facts, as I unearth them and put them together.'

'But what about The Crawler: is he or is he not in the frame?'

'I don't know anything about "The Crawler", Bob. I bow to your expertise on that subject. It was you and your mates who made him up.'

'So, you are not taking seriously or considering the eyewitness reports of the man, and the car, that have been placed at the scene of two of the three previous murders? Shouldn't that be your priority? Isn't that your job?'

'My job is to go carefully through the facts of the case and follow any leads as they emerge, not fuel endless, pointless speculation at these pantomime press conferences. Your job, Bob, as far as I can tell, is to intrude into the lives and exploit the grief of people who've just had their daughters brutally murdered, and make up ridiculous damn stories about serial murderers. Come back to me when you've got some actual, solid facts to talk about. Next question.'

Amanda Gregory of the *Daily Mail* raised her hand from the front row and caught H's eye before anyone else could. She was just about the most aggressive and sarcastic of the lot, but she carried a lot of clout and couldn't be ignored. H liked to get her out of the way early on.

'This talk of jobs and roles and professionalism seems very pertinent, DI Hawkins. What do you have to say about the photos that appeared in my paper on Wednesday of you falling out of a Soho drinking club at two o'clock in the morning? On a Tuesday? With the bodies of young girls piling up quicker than you can count them?'

'Nothing.'

'Nothing at all, to satisfy my readers, and the country at large, that you are doing everything within your power to bring this situation under control?'

'I was in a meeting. I conduct my business as I see fit.'

'Until two o'clock?'

'I don't need a lot of sleep. I've got a very active mind and a lot of energy, and I like to keep busy. I'm a bit like Mrs. Thatcher in that respect. Anyway, enough about me. Next question.'

'Big admirer of the Iron Lady, are you DI Hawkins?' shouted Norman Bishop of the *Daily Mirror*, above the rising hubbub.

'Not relevant. Next question.'

Budgie McAllister quietly entered the room, H noticed in his peripheral vision, through a side door.

H invited a question from Michael Pike of ITV News, which he hoped might be a little more measured; he was already tired of the Punch and Judy stuff.

'Can you confirm,' asked Pike, 'that the most recent victim had come down to London from the North recently, like two of the others? My sources tell me as much.'

'Yes, Martina Pallister came down from Bolton. She seems to have arrived in London about two weeks ago, as far as we can tell. As for what you say about "the others", it's not yet clear that these cases are linked.'

'But you are keeping an open mind on the matter?'

'I am.'

'Good to hear he's keeping an open mind on something', said the man from the *Mirror*, to appreciative laughter from those around him.'

This did not go unnoticed on the podium.

'You got something to say to me Bishop? Or are you just having a little whispering party with the other girls?'

The Chief Superintendent placed his hand on H's forearm, and whispered into his ear: 'Not now H, please.

14

You've done a grand job so far. Don't let that little bastard rattle you.'

'I'm not rattled, guvnor, I…'

'Enough, H. Time to draw proceedings to a close, I think. DS McAllister looks like he has a message for you – this would be a good time to take it.'

H nodded and beckoned the young man to the podium, ignoring the rising tide of chatter and jostle in the room.

'What is it, Budge?'

McAllister handed him a note: *We've found another body.*

# 1pm

For the first time in his career, H had found a press conference almost to be a relief. True enough, his bile was rising, and it was about to start getting out of hand when the guvnor had intervened, but compared to what was coming next it was a quiet stroll, in a beautiful park on a sunny day.

Budgie McAllister brought him up to speed in the car; they were bound for Tooting Common in the south west of the city. They'd been sitting on the obvious similarities in the murders of the girls for weeks, until they had something more solid to go public with. But this new one, H already knew in his gut, would turn out to be the fifth in the sequence. Budgie wouldn't have come to him during a press conference otherwise.

'It sounds like an absolute dog's dinner down there, guvnor. Young girl in all sorts of a mess. Found under some bushes on Tooting Common, not far from the red-light area there.'

'What do we know about that area, Budge? Mostly kerb-crawlers and girls just right out there on the street, no?'

'Yep, and it's been getting busier and busier down there. I spoke to a mate in Vice and he tells me it's blowing up because a lot of girls are getting edged out of or are escaping from Soho. A lot of them are getting caught between a rock and a hard place – Albanian pimps taking control on the one hand, Westminster Council trying to shut down the sex trade on the other. One of their periodical purges. Have you seen the property prices there lately? Urban regeneration, I think they call it.'

'Yeah, I know. Money talking, I call it. Business as usual, with these poor kids as the shit in the sandwich. And now some sick, perverted nutter on the rampage to contend with by the looks of it, as if they haven't got enough to worry about. Forensics down there already?'

'Yep. They should be well underway by the time we get there.'

H took another hit on his flask and readied himself for what was coming.

\*\*\*

The Common was buzzing, with PCs holding the perimeter line against rubberneckers and media people and, inside, the forensics people milling about like archaeologists at a dig. At the centre of things was the quiet but unmissable figure of Sebastian Kinsella. H had never liked him much – he was one of those wacky, otherworldly characters straight out of central casting that the makers of TV crime dramas seemed to love – but he knew his stuff and was now, after just a few years in the saddle, one of the top forensic specialists in the Met.

'Talk to me Baz,' said H, 'do I have to inspect the body myself or does it fit with the others?'

'Becoming sensitive in your old age, DI Hawkins?'

'I'm not in the mood, son. Speak to me.'

'Well, it's either the same perpetrator as the others or as good a copycat as I've ever seen. The eyes have been gouged out, as usual, and there's the same terrible mess down below. As with the others it's difficult to say what the sequence was, but the same *modus operandi*. Savagely raped, brutalized with a knife down below after the act, and blinded, probably with the same knife.'

'Anything else we need to know?' said H.

'Indeed there is, Detective Inspector Hawkins, indeed there is. She was covered in cigarette burns, of various vintages, welts across the back indicating a series of thrashings with what was probably a bamboo cane. These go back a few months, I'd say. At any rate, all of these wounds were inflicted upon the poor girl well before last evening.'

'Evidence?'

'We're picking up the usual samples – he's left plenty of semen about. I'll be able to let you know if it, and the sample from last night's girl, match the previous three tomorrow. If they do, your problems with "The Crawler" are only just beginning.'

H thanked Kinsella, turned on his heels and headed back to the car, by way of Budgie McAllister, who was ferreting about in the bushes. 'I'll be in the motor, Budge,' he said quietly. 'Get a look at her effects if there are any – before forensics takes them away. This bastard's taking the piss out of us, and I've had enough. I don't want to sit about all night waiting for the lab to finish with everything. See if you can get a peek.'

H sat and watched his DS from the car, ducking and diving and looking at bits and pieces and making notes. It looked like the kid was getting his teeth into things. Lovely. H ducked down under the dashboard, pulled out his flask and drained it.

The need to sleep overtook him; his eyelids fell under the weight of it and he fell into fitful half-nightmare visions of hairy monsters lurking in colons and the eye-gouged death masks of pretty girls. Budgie McAllister pulled him back to reality with a tap on the window and a vigorous pulling open of the car door.

'Right, guvnor,' he said excitedly, 'we've got something to get our teeth into. At fucking last. We need to head for Soho.'

'Tell me more, my son...tell me more,' said H, sparking up the ignition.

Budgie flipped open his notebook. 'Right, I got a look inside her little clutch bag thingy, and found items of interest. First up, she's not from the North or Scotland, she's from Russia or Ukraine, somewhere like that. Cyrillic writing on her ID card. But judging from the date she's 19. Her name was Yulia.'

'How do we know that, if it was all written in double-Dutch?'

'There was one other thing, among the lipstick and condoms – a flyer, with some writing on the back addressed to "Yulia" from someone described on the front of the flyer as the rector of St Anne's church in Soho – you know, off Dean Street, at the Shaftesbury Avenue end. Name of Margaret Possiter.'

'And what did it say, the note on the back of the flyer?' asked H.

'Hope you can make it, Yulia. Love, Margaret P.'

'And the flyer?'

'" Hello all, just to let you know the next meeting of the Soho Sex Workers' collective is on October 27th at 8 pm, in the church hall. We're starting early so anyone who is working outside can try and come along. Things are really cooking here now, there's a lot happening. Do try and make it, we need as many people to attend as possible." All of this superimposed on a grainy old picture of the church exterior.'

'OK. Nothing else of interest in the bag?'

'Nope.'

'Right, let's go and have a word with the rector,' said H.

# 4.30pm

They pulled into Soho around four o'clock just as the daylight, such as it was, was fading. The area had always been like a second home to H, for whom it was as much of a playground as a workplace. Soho still kept the Met busy; the sex trade, the takeover of almost all serious criminal activity by organized Eastern European gangs, the theatre-goers mugged and robbed, the packs of drunken lads down from the North, the waifs and strays and tourists getting themselves into trouble…no matter how hard the authorities tried to tame and polish it, the dark heart of Soho was still beating.

But St Anne's church was a first. Neither business nor pleasure had brought it into focus for him before. He was not much familiar with churches; it was not that they bothered him, he'd just felt all of his adult life that they were not for him. He felt no anti-religious animus towards the church. A couple of years of Sunday school in Bermondsey as a small boy at his mother's insistence had equipped him with knowledge of the headline bible stories, and he'd always liked the Old Testament. But church was just for weddings and funerals, not for him.

They found Margaret Possiter outside, tending to a tomb in the tiny churchyard. She was not the militant feminist harridan H had been expecting, but a charming, grey-haired gentlewoman in her late-sixties or early-seventies.

They asked her about Yulia, and the flyer, and gave her the news. She dropped the trowel she was holding onto the ground and fell back on to her haunches. It was colder now, and darker, and she pulled her outsized multi-coloured cardigan around herself more tightly.

'Dear Lord, when will it end? That poor, sweet girl,' she said. 'Is it linked to these other killings?'

'We think so, yes,' said H.

He allowed a long silence to develop; Margaret Possiter was clearly having trouble coming to terms with what she'd heard.

'So,' he said presently, 'what can you tell us about her? It's very important that we build up a picture of her life, her contacts. You're the first person we've found with a solid link to any of these girls.'

'Yes, of course. Why don't we go inside? I'll make some tea.'

She led them into a building next to the church and began pottering about in its small kitchen while they stood in the doorway.

'If we could start with any biographical information you may have about her,' said Budgie.

'Well, her name was Yulia Pankevich. She was from Belarus, a place called Vitebsk. She told me quite a bit about it, and her childhood there.'

'So you spent a fair bit of time with her then?' said H.

'Yes, she came here a few times, during the day, and we chatted. This is the only church in the area, and she was religious. Orthodox, as they are there. I find a lot of the Eastern European girls are drawn to the church. A good number of them come here, and confide in me. I think I remind them of their aunts back home.'

'So, you've got a pretty good overview of how they live, and what's what?' said Budgie.

'Yes, DS McAllister, I'm afraid I have – I'm very much afraid I have.'

'Were you familiar with any of the other murdered girls that have been in the news?' asked H.

'No, she would be the first. I've been following events quite closely, and haven't recognised anyone. I don't think they were all Soho girls.'

'What makes you say that?' asked Budgie.

21

'Well, the girls caught up in the game here tend to be an international bunch – Eastern Europeans, Africans, Indians, all sorts. They tend to have been brought in through trafficking, and locked into the organized activities here. The girls who've been in the news look to me more like British waifs and strays – so, you know...not connected to Soho.'

'Any idea when Yulia arrived here?' said H. 'When did you meet her?'

'Around the beginning of the year, I think. I met her in February, around that time, and she came here a fair bit, when she wasn't in lockdown.'

'Lockdown?' said Budgie.

'Yes, I mean when their controllers punish them for going off-track or doing what they shouldn't – like coming here. They keep most of them inside most of the time anyway. The compliant ones are let out from time to time, but any disobedience results, effectively, in house-arrest. Things can get very ugly for them then.'

'Yes, we know Margaret – they are kept as slaves and suffer foul abuse,' said H. 'What about Yulia, did she get plenty of that?'

'Yes, she seemed to draw the worst out of them. Which is saying something. She was so pretty, and young, and vulnerable – there was no hardness in her. And she was blonde. A dangerous combination of characteristics to have around here.'

'Why so, exactly?' asked Budgie.

'Because their pimps – I should say "owners" – are now almost exclusively Albanian...'

'The significance of which is?' said Budgie.

'Ah, I see you are not experienced in working vice cases, DS McAllister. Well, the significance is they treat the women they command as if they were subhuman, just things. And they have a penchant for blonde women.'

'And Yulia?' said H.

'She came along here a few weeks back, very distraught. She said she couldn't take much more. I offered to take her out of the area, to a safe house. But they get a kind of Stockholm Syndrome – these men may be savages, but they have cunning; they know how to turn a girl and make her reliant on them.'

The realities of what Yulia Pankevich had been through hit H hard. He bit his tongue. His jaw ached from his clenching of it since the moment they'd arrived at Tooting Common.

'Yes, Detective Inspector Hawkins, it's even worse than you think,' said Margaret Possiter. 'And for full disclosure, I must tell you that on that last visit she showed me her wounds: welt marks across her back from canings, cigarette burns around her thighs and breasts. I wept for pity and begged her to let me get her out, but…'

'Jesus fucking Christ,' shouted H, beginning to lose control of his emotions. 'If you will excuse my French, Margaret, and the taking of the Lord's name in vain. Exactly where are these people?'

'That I don't know with any degree of accuracy, I'm afraid. You'd do well to consult your vice people – I'm sure they can dot the i's and cross the t's for you.'

'Alright Margaret, thanks for your help. We're sorry to have been the bearers of such miserable tidings. One last thing: did Yulia ever mention any names, in connection with what you've just told us?'

'No, her lips were sealed. Never a name. That was rule number one – never any names.'

# 6pm

The two of them trudged back down Dean Street in the never-ending rain, H saying very little. Budgie observed unusual body language coming from the big man; his head was down, his face muscles taut and his jaw grinding; there was none of the usual zip in him. He was exuding intense negative energy. Budgie had never seen him like this before, and it unnerved him. He broke the silence as they turned into Old Compton Street.

'Well, it's a sick world and no mistake, skipper.'

'No arguments there, Budge.'

'No. So what's next, where to?'

'I need a drink.'

'Now?'

'Yes, nothing major. Just a quick one – I need to be home at eight, I've got to deal with the kids.'

'OK, where d'you fancy, French House?'

'Fuck the French House. I am not in the mood to sit around watching fashion students sipping white wine.'

'Coach and Horses?'

'Nah, not any more…it's always full of tourists looking for local "characters" these days.'

'Skipper, the rain's not easing up any. Can we just slip inside somewhere and dry out?'

'OK, sorry Budge. Let's get in the Pillar of Hercules.'

'Not familiar with…'

'Greek Street, Budge. Greek Street. Follow me.'

Budgie did as he was told, and traipsed after H's brooding hulk in watery, rapidly descending early evening gloom. It was like walking underwater, at the bottom of a deep sea scarcely penetrated by light.

H and his elemental surroundings, Budgie observed as they suddenly swung right on Greek Street and barrelled into the Pillar of Hercules' quiet interior, were perfectly matched. This observation was no less true of the under-lit, higgledy-piggledy interior of the pub. H removed his raincoat, took a corner table and placed his order.

'Pint of whatever proper beer they've got and a double scotch please Budge. And don't let the grass grow under your feet, son – I am absolutely fucking gagging here.'

Budgie returned from the bar muttering about surly Eastern European barmen; he was picking up on H's mood, being drawn into a dark and malcontent emotional space. H sank both the drinks he'd delivered before Budgie had managed to get his hand around his pint of lager, and said 'Right Budge, same again?'

'I'm alright with this one at the minute, skipper.'

H went to the bar and returned with two pints and two scotch chasers.

'There you are, Budge – get these down you son, they'll do you the power of good,' he said.

'Thanks boss, but I need to take it steady – I have a three-pint limit on working days.'

'Three-pint limit? What are you, a man or a mouse?'

'I'm a man skipper – a man who likes to keep himself in order during the week. I only go on the lash at the weekends now. I've had a few issues.'

'"Issues"? What are you fucking talking about – "Issues"? You mean "problems'? What does a wet-behind-the-ears, great long streak of piss like you know about problems?'

H drank his pint and chased it with his scotch, pushed the glasses away, and dragged Budgie's untouched second lager and scotch across the table to his own pitch.

'You want to talk about issues? Try this: I've been dealing with the dirty, evil, murderous scum of the earth now for donkey's years, and never taken a day off work. Never had any fucking "issues" with that. I've been looking at bodies like Yulia Pankevich's for all that time, and tracking down

25

the dirty pieces of shit that ruined them. Day in, day out. Looking them in the eye and making them pay. That's what we're paid for, Budge – tracking down evil bastards and trying to protect the Yulia Pankeviches of this world.'

'Yes skipper, I know. I was only...'

'Only what? Getting ready to tell me about your "issues"? What is it with you young blokes? Always having "issues", unable to cope, taking months off work on the sick because the job's made you feel bad.'

'Skipper, I have not had one fucking day off on the sick since I came on the job. I've not pulled a single stroke like that...Why are you making me into your straw man?'

H said nothing, and fixed Budgie with a hard stare and a clenched jaw. The younger man saw, with astonishment, that the big man's eyes were watery and red, as if he were on the verge of crying.

H went to the bar again and returned with his usual, and a bag of peanuts.

'There you go, Budge. Peace offering. Nice bit of protein for you. Apologies for going off like that – nothing to do with you really. I've got a few things on my mind.'

They fell to silence for a minute or two, while H disappeared into some sort of reverie. Budgie waited it out.

H returned to the present.

'Go get the drinks in Budge, I've got an idea.'

Budgie went back to the bar, ordered the round and did a little mental arithmetic while the barman fiddled with the pump. They'd been in the place less than an hour; Budgie calculated that H had already sunk three pints of beer and one of lager, and four double scotches. This was on top of whatever he'd had earlier in the day and his frequent hits on his pocket flask. Where did he put it all? And why did he never seem drunk, but just more intense?

'OK skipper,' said Budgie back at the table, 'what's your idea?'

'Let's go and root about where the Albanians hang out. We know more or less where to look for them. Let's go and straighten a few out – see how they go with men who bite back, rather than the little girls they like to terrorise. Let's see what they're made of.'

'That is a *very* bad idea boss.'

'Why? What's the matter Budge, not got the arsehole for it? I thought you were supposed to be a Glasgow boy.'

'Well, for starters we'd get into a shitload of trouble if someone finds out. Plus they're bound to be well tooled-up, and we're holding nothing. And second, Vice have been running surveillance on them and building a case for months. Years, for all we know.'

'Tell that to Yulia Pankevich's mum and dad.'

'So, what you really want to do is avenge their loss?'

'Yep, don't you?'

'Yes, but…the best way to do that is gather evidence, put it all through the system, close them down for ever.'

'There's no closing these fuckers down for ever Budge. We build a case and raid them, some snidey human rights lawyer gets involved, they end up with a little seven-stretch, making a fortune dealing drugs in the nick because the screws are terrified of them. It never ends, Budge, you know that.'

Budgie sighed heavily, sipped his beer and kept his own counsel.

'So, what you're saying, DS McAllister, is that if I want to go in there now I've got to fly solo. Yes?'

'Skipper, I never said I wouldn't back you up. What I said was it's a terrible idea…But if you're intent on wading in somewhere, and causing mayhem, and getting yourself cut to pieces or blown to kingdom come, and maybe ruining your career, and probably mine…'

'You're in.'

'Of course I fucking am.'

'Good man, I knew I could count on you. I was only joking...same again? said H as he got up and headed for the bar.

*** 

The session wore on, with H doing his best to drink the Pillars of Hercules dry, and the evening crowd arrived. By nine o'clock the trips to the bar were taking longer, and on one return to the table Budgie thought he saw H wipe a tear away from the corner of an eye. By now he understood that something very serious was afoot for H, and knew also that he was unlikely to be told what it was no matter how many drinks the skipper threw down his gullet.

But the big man was, at last, getting woozy. It had taken enough booze to stun an elephant to get him there, but he was definitely getting woozy. Budgie spotted his chance.

'Shall we make this the last one then skipper – you said you had to be home by eight, and it's nine now. Let's just sink these and I'll run you home.'

'But you've been drinking, DC McAllister.'

'We'll jump in a cab. My shout.'

'Jump in a cab? To Eltham? On your wages? Nah, I've got a better idea than that, Budge. Let's go to Ronnie Scott's and have a proper drink. Come on son, you know it makes sense.'

If Budgie McAllister had more time, and the situation was not so close to getting out of control, he might have tried to calculate the amount of alcohol H would have to consume before he was satisfied he was having a proper drink. But that was for another time; Budgie drove the point home.

'Listen, skipper: you've had a skinful already, and your kids are waiting for you. You said Julie's going out and you have to get home, so that's where I'm going to take you. Drink up. Don't argue with me now boss...drink up.'

28

# 10pm

Julie heard the cab pull into the driveway. He was two hours late – nothing unusual in that, but tonight of all nights…

She clicked the TV off, took a deep breath, did her best to suppress her rage, and her stomach-churning despair, and opened the front door. Her husband, supported by Budgie McAllister, looked a little unsteady on his feet but seemed compos mentis, more or less. Julie took all this in at a glance. She'd had plenty of practice.

She did not address H directly, nor meet his eye. 'Cup of tea or something for you Budge, before I go?'

'No, you're alright Mrs. Hawkins, thanks. I'll just park the big man here on your sofa, if I may, and jump back in the cab. Early start in the morning.'

'Yes, I bet you have, with another one of these poor girls getting murdered. Deptford…They seem to be getting closer and closer. It's terrible.'

'Deptford?', said Budgie, 'when?"

'Well, it was just on the news – they said her body was discovered this evening. You didn't know?'

'No, I've been in the pub with H. You know what he's like with mobile phones. He didn't have his with him and he takes a dim view of me getting mine out when we're drinking, so I had it switched off.'

'Well, the bloody great lump doesn't look like he'll be much use to you in the morning…Good night Budge, thanks for bringing him. For what he's worth.'

'Night Mrs. H,' said Budgie with a wan smile, before barrelling out of the door and back to the cab.

Julie went to the kitchen, made strong coffee and brought it back to the slumbering hulk on the sofa.

'H. H! Wake up you bastard, and drink the coffee. Come on, liven up, you know I'm going out. Don't let me down tonight, H. I'm going to spend the night at Justin's. As we agreed. You are, you *were*, going to talk to the kids and put them in the picture. They're asleep now...you'll have to do it in the morning.'

H made a snuffling sound, but his eyes remained closed.

'H! Wake up, you drunken bastard,' Julie screamed, clawing at his collar and shoulders and accidentally spilling coffee on his overcoat.

H came round and saw – really saw – the person known to him as his wife, or soon to be his ex-wife, as if for the first time in an age. He saw her tears and her desperately contorted features and felt himself engulfed by the accumulated distress, disappointment and unhappiness of many years. How had it come to this? What had he done to her? What would he do now?

'Drink your coffee H,' Julie snarled. 'Just fucking drink it. I'm not going to sit here and shout at you and argue with you. We're way beyond all that now. You know what's happening – get your head out of your arse and look at what's happening to your life...What's happened to your family. Just fucking face up to it, finally.'

H opened his eyes wider, and sat upright, and took it all in wordlessly, as he had so many times before.

'I'm going now, and you have to talk to the children. If you can't even do this, for them, I'll cut you out and you'll never see them again. Do you understand? Me and Justin will make sure you never see them again, unless you just fucking shape up for once.'

H nodded, blearily, but still said nothing.

'Speak to them. I'll be back in the morning.'

Julie left the room. H sat in his usual stunned silence, letting the awareness of what was happening, and what needed to be done, seep out of his gut and into his head. H heard Julie bustle about in the bathroom, then come back along the passage to put on her coat, then check her face in the mirror and fiddle with her handbag, then slam the front door, then open and slam the car door, then spark up the engine and pull slowly out of their little driveway.

\*\*\*

He awoke on the sofa. It was two-thirty in the morning, a little short of the witching hour. He tried to figure out where he was, but found himself crying uncontrollably before he could. It came to him. The pain in his stomach threatened to overwhelm him; he felt around on the floor for his coffee, took a gulp, and a deep breath, and forced himself to his feet.

His slow trudge up the stairs to the children's rooms felt like the walk of destiny – like a specific kind of journey he would make only once, and recall with regret for the rest of his life. His knees were buckling under him, and the bitter tears continued to fall from his face, but he stifled his sobbing. He would tell the kids, but he wouldn't wake them up. Not properly. He went into Grace's room and lifted her tiny figure from the bed as gently as he could. He carried her into Little Ronnie's room on tiptoe, holding his breath, making only very small sounds. He eased the boy across his bed to make room for his sister, and put her down with her head on the available half of the pillow.

He stood up and stepped back from the bed, shrugging off his overcoat as he did so. He examined their faces in the half-light cast into the room by the lamp post in the street outside, and found himself lingering on Grace's face. It began to merge with the pictures he'd seen of some of the dead girls, before their little-girl beauty had been so foully desecrated. What was to become of her, his little girl?

He fell to his knees, and bowed his head as if to pray. But he didn't pray, he simply allowed his hungover mind to wander where it would. It took him nowhere good, or

31

inspiring, simply through spiralling nightmare images of disfigured bodies, sneering murderers, dead soldiers, the face of his crying wife begging him to change, reeling, kaleidoscopic scenes of extreme drunkenness and his countless late nights out on the town, on the missing list. It was his lot, it had always been his lot, to carry the weight of the evil of others on his shoulders.

He shook his head to make it stop and focused again on Little Ronnie and Grace and finally summoned up the courage – hollow and gnarled as he felt – to do what he'd come to do.

'Listen kids,' he whispered, 'I've got to tell you something. Something important. Daddy and mummy have had a big fight – a lot of big fights…with words. Word fights. Now mummy says she doesn't want daddy to live here in our house any more, and I have to go away. I won't go far – I have a place round here, so you can come and see me whenever you want. And I'll still be your daddy…I'll always be your daddy, and I'll always love you. I just won't live with you anymore. So, tomorrow will be the first day of me not living with you anymore, and…'

There was nothing more he could say. He kissed them both tenderly on the forehead. He was sobbing quietly now and wanted to climb into bed with them, to hold them for one last time, in this house, where they had all been together, but saw that the best he could do would be to hunker down on the floor next to the bed instead. He rolled his overcoat into a pillow, stretched his weary self out and, with his arm stretched up and across his children as far as he could get it, fell asleep.

# Counter Punch

# October 1984

Rita forced her way onto the busy roundabout at the Elephant and Castle, navigated the throngs of lane-switching traffic and edged her way slowly across the road before taking the exit onto the New Kent Road, all the while wondering why she still took her dad to fights: he was beaten to within an inch of his life in the last one.

Her dad, Jimmy, known as 'Rottweiler' to many of those who populated the seedier pubs of south east London, sat in the back seat hugging two of his massive canine namesakes, drawing courage and strength from their powerful innocence. Her dad was all but a lost cause, thought Rita, as she picked her way over the Bricklayers Arms flyover and down into The Old Kent Road.

It was a cold November night, but the pubs and clubs along and around the Old Kent Road were as lively as ever; now, at eleven o'clock, revellers were pouring out of their drinking dens under cover of darkness. The evening would shortly spark into life with the usual Friday night street brawls and police sirens. Many of those who didn't get picked up by the initial sweep of the meat wagons would be making their way to the abandoned warehouse in Rolls Road in which Jimmy 'Rottweiler' Jefferson would soon be plying his trade.

Rita winced at the thought of it. She knew her dad was getting too old and too weak for this. They'd had a hundred arguments, but he remained adamant. 'It's what I do babe. We need the money. It's all I know how to do.' His stubbornness was legendary, and she always gave up, in the end. When push came to shove she always found herself waiting outside some obscure venue while a hungry young buck smashed seven shades out of her father. In the early days, when she was a little girl, it had been different. He was

36

a force to be reckoned with then, a local legend who usually won and returned home with no more than a few scratches and a big wad of cash. It had paid for holidays in Spain and fabulous days out at the Tower of London, Thorpe Park, London Zoo, Leeds Castle. But not anymore. Now he always lost.

She didn't believe his arguments about needing the money – they were a smokescreen. Bare-knuckle fighting was a life, she knew, he would never be able to give up, even if he won the pools. It was the life that validated him, made him someone. What it would take, short of death itself, to make him stop was a question that preoccupied her day after day.

Outside the sirens had started wailing and the dark night closed in on them. Inside the car no words were exchanged. The atmosphere was tense and claustrophobic. Jimmy lit up a cigarette, took a long drag and released his tension with a slow exhale of breath and smoke through his nose. A crowd was already forming when they arrived. Bloodlust was in the air. Rita swallowed her nausea as she got out of the car and said hello to Lennie Prentice, the fight promoter – a sharp-suited, good-looking and no-nonsense force of nature who was a major player on multiple fronts in this part of the world. He'd always had a soft spot for Rita and welcomed her with his big lord-of-all-he-surveyed promotor hug.

'Hello darling, how you doing? Hope the old boy's up for it tonight, he's facing Eddie 'No Surrender' McKinley. This boy's been smashing all-comers in West London for the last couple of months.' Rita barely acknowledged him, except to say 'Well, Len, this ain't West London, is it?' The nausea in the pit of her stomach intensified when her father stepped out of the car and was embraced and led away by Prentice and his people.

'Coming in to watch?' said Prentice, looking over his shoulder and eyeing up her fine figure.

'No. Bring him out when it's done. I'll be here.'

She knew her father was there to take a beating, to give the younger fighter another victory, to build his momentum and roll his reputation on. It didn't matter that The Rottweiler hadn't won a fight in ages; his old reputation was still enough to give some gloss to the up-and-comers. Rita's father was now no more than a punch bag. She hated this game and everyone in it, especially the promoters and the bookies, the experts in the art of drawing in a crowd of drunken young men to scam in the betting.

She sat in the back of the car and waited for the fight to begin, and when it did she grimaced at each crescendo of the screaming crowd, bound together by the bloodlust, jeering and exulting in unison at the humiliation and physical destruction of her father. She wondered where their need for violence came from as she hugged the dogs for strength and consolation, as her father had done just before the fight, and prayed that the damage he suffered this time round would not be catastrophic.

Ten minutes later it became apparent that her prayers had not been answered. She looked on in horror as two of Prentice's minders burst out of the warehouse and poured her father into the back of the car. She could see at a glance that he had a broken nose for sure, almost completely closed eyes, and was coughing up thick, bloody knots of phlegm. She acknowledged the minders with polite contempt in her eyes as the dogs jumped on their master and licked excitedly at his wounds. Prentice was nowhere to be seen; he would still be inside, counting his money. 'You better get your old man round to the doc, sharpish,' said one of the minders, 'he's taken a proper hammering.'

***

It was a small place, just a few streets away, with old Doc Rolfe in attendance as usual. He was wizened and world-weary but also kind and caring, and did his best to put The Rottweiler back together. When the cleansing and stitching was done he gave Rita a script for super-strength painkillers, and helped her get him established as comfortably as possible on the back seat.

'I know I've said this to you before, Ree,' said Doc Rolfe when they'd finally got the car door closed, 'but you've got to stop him fighting. The next one will very likely kill him. I'm giving you a note for the hospital – make an appointment at Guy's and take him to get his brain scanned. You've got to find a way of stopping him. I don't want you bringing him here after a fight again – it's all getting too near the knuckle for me now. I can't have him dying on me here.'

Rita drove back to their flat on the Aylesbury Estate in Walworth, via an all-night chemist in the New Kent Road, with the doctor's words ringing in her ears so loud she couldn't hear herself think. She managed to bundle her dad out of the car, with plenty of vocal encouragement and to-ing and fro-ing from the dogs, into the lift and onto his bed before collapsing with exhaustion.

She woke up early, in the chair she'd slumped down into, and popped her head round her dad's bedroom door. He was awake, and emitting low groans. At least he was alive. She took him a cup of strong tea and two of the painkillers. She asked him if he wanted any breakfast, which he declined by raising the volume of his grunts and groans.

She sat on the edge of the bed and felt his forehead, and began to cry. 'This is it dad. The last time. I'm not taking you anymore and if you fight again I'm leaving. Like mum did. And I won't come back, again, ever, like her. You'll be on your own, with just the dogs to see you out…you'll die here on your own.'

'Hello Ree,' said H as he opened the door of his parent's flat off Raymouth Road. H was delighted to see his old friend – his cousin, really; their families had always been close and they'd enjoyed an intense platonic friendship since early childhood. This was their first meeting since H was stationed in West Germany; this was his first spell of leave in what seemed an age.

Rita was surprised by the difference in him since their last meeting, the sight of him stirred something in her that hadn't been there before, or that she had never been aware of, or had just suppressed. He was so tall and strong, so proud, and…sexy. A young warrior in his prime, tall and upright and bursting with manly vigour.

He embraced her warmly, and it was as much as she could do to say 'Hello H. I heard you were on leave. My God, you look well. All that soldiering seems to be doing you the power of good.'

'Yeah, it's a good life. I'm just here for a couple of weeks, then off to Northern Ireland for another tour there.'

They went upstairs to the kitchen and H made tea. They chatted amiably enough for a couple of minutes, and brought each other up to speed, but he could tell that Rita – who was not looking so bad herself, in her fully-developed mid-20s – was troubled by something.

'So, to what do I owe the pleasure of the visit Ree? Anything in particular?'

'It's dad,' said Rita, 'he had another fight last week. He's in a shocking state. Absolutely shocking.'

'I thought he'd turned it in – he's way too old for all that palaver.'

'That's the thing H, he can't give it up. He says it's the only way of putting food on the table. We can get by, but he just won't stop.'

'Who's he fighting for? I mean who puts the fights on these days?'

'Lenny Prentice.'

'That no-good bastard still controlling this, is he? Your dad's made him a lot of money over the years.'

'I know. Now he's just using dad as a punch bag for up and coming fighters.'

Rita shuddered at the thought, and got ready to cry. She'd been crying a lot recently. H held her tight; he made her feel safe, and she calmed down.

'Want me to have a word with The Rottweiler?'

'Would you? Someone has to try and convince him he's got to stop.'

'No problem,' said H as he passed Rita her tea; only now did she notice the third cup.

'I thought your mum and dad were out today. Is Julie here?' said Rita with a wry smile, recovering her composure, 'you really should marry that girl before she leaves you.'

H smiled. Rita was right, of course. 'Julie's not going to leave me, don't you worry about that. We're getting married as soon as I come out of the army. In just over a year – it's all sorted. But no, the tea's not for her – I've got a mate staying with me. Come into the front room, I'll introduce you.'

H picked up two cups and bowled out of the kitchen and into the living room.

'Rita, this is Chuck. Chuck Vaughan. Chuck, this is Rita.'

'Well, hello ma'am,' said Chuck, drawing out the "ma'am" suggestively, rising from his chair and extending a hand. 'It sure is a pleasure to meet you,' he drawled in the kind of Texas accent she'd only ever heard before in films.

'Hello Chuck, nice to meet you.'

'Chuck's from the good old USA,' said H, unnecessarily. 'We've been working together in West Germany. He wanted to see the sights of London, so he's come over for the weekend.'

Chuck, much to Rita's delight, was straight out of central casting: crewcut, piercing blue eyes, square jaw, broad shoulders above pumped-up arms, and protruding chest. Rita imagined the washboard stomach under the tight white t-shirt, and gave him her most coquettish smile.

'An American in London… You're a long way from home, Chuck.'

'Yeah. But I have H to look after me.'

'You don't look like you need a lot of looking after.'

'Well thank you ma'am, I'll take that as a compliment.'

'Ree, we're going uptown later,' said H. 'You know, Trafalgar Square and all that. Fancy it?'

Rita didn't want to appear over-eager in her response to the invitation, but she did, and didn't care. Something about the looks Chuck was giving her made her not care.

'Yeah, sure, why not?'

'Right,' said H. 'I'll leave you two to it for bit and go round and see the old man now. I'll be an hour or two, we can get going when I get back. You better give me your front door keys Ree, I don't want to drag him out of bed.'

H reminisced, while he drove to the Walworth Road, about Jimmy and Irene Jefferson, and his own mum and dad and the circle of friends who were always around when he and his brothers were little. They always seemed to be having parties, laughing and joking and singing deep into the night at weekends, keeping him awake. Sinatra and Dean Martin, and other songs. *Maybe It's Because I'm A Londoner. Show Me The Way To Go Home.* He had nothing but fond memories of those days of his childhood. Jimmy was one of many full-on, larger-than-life big characters, like his dad.

But the wrecked, utterly forlorn figure he found lying in bed shocked him. H hadn't seen him for a few years, and the giant had shrunk, and withered, and now looked weak and vulnerable and…pathetic. The beating he'd recently received just made it worse. It was heart breaking; Jimmy Jefferson was a pale shadow of his former self. H propped him up on the pillows, made him a cup of tea, and set out the case he'd come to make on Rita's behalf.

Jimmy heard him out, pulled himself upright as best he could and summoned up the energy for a reply.

'Listen H, you're a good kid. I've always had time for you. Your old man as well. But don't think you can stroll in here and start telling me how to live my fucking life. Who do you think you are? I can still remember you in short trousers.'

H had come with the best of intentions, full of respect and quiet concern. But *The Rottweiler* was digging in, like one of his dogs with a bone, and talking to H like he was some sort of idiot started a chain reaction, and there was now no stopping it.

'Jim, I'm telling you you're too fucking old for all that bollocks. It's as plain as the broken nose on your mashed-up face. You can't compete with these young blokes anymore. Face up to it mate, you're going to get yourself killed if you keep going, or even worse wind up as some sort of basket-case who has to be spoon fed by Rita for the rest of your fucking life. What about her? Have you even thought about her?'

'Get out.'

'Think about it. Is that the future you want for her? Being a bit selfish ain't you?'

'I said get the fuck out, now. Make sure you close the door on your way.'

\*\*\*

H avoided talking about his encounter with the old man while the three of them were out; he wanted Rita and Chuck to enjoy their trip. It was a gloomy but mild afternoon and

43

they walked from Trafalgar Square up Charing Cross Road and into Leicester square, then up into Oxford Street, all the way along to Marble Arch and into Hyde Park. Rita, who had been a studious pupil at school and knew a lot about London's West End and its history, played tour guide. Chuck ate it up, and begged for more. The two of them got on like a house on fire, which suited H; his meeting with what was left of Jimmy Jefferson had left him in a sombre and reflective mood.

When they were all walked-out H suggested they go for a drink, so they took a cab back to Soho and set themselves up in the upstairs bar of a pub on Cambridge Circus. H set the pace and Chuck matched him beer-for-beer, once he got used to its being warm and flat; but he couldn't do anything about the punch it delivered – these were strong drinks, much stronger than the fizzy yellow ones he was used to, and they caught up with him quickly. It hit him seven pints in, and he rose unsteadily to his feet and staggered to the toilet for what looked like might be a lengthy stay.

'OK Ree, about your dad,' said H. 'I did what I could with him, but he's got to be the most stubborn bastard I've ever come across. He won't listen to reason. I think he's probably punchy. I'd get the hospital to have a look at his brain if I was you. A few more good clumps to the head, and…'

'We've got an appointment, H. At Guy's. It'll probably take two or three months, old Doc Rolfe said.'

'Let's hope that's not too long,' said H.

'But I think he's stable…not in any immediate danger?'

'I don't know, Ree, not for me to say. I'd be more concerned about the danger from Prentice – he might want to put him in another fight in that timeframe.'

'I don't see how, H. You saw him yourself – he's in a terrible state. What sort of a fight could he put up now, in the state he's in?'

'Ree, it's not about that. In a month or two, as long as he can get himself on his feet and put his hands up, I wouldn't be surprised if Prentice laid something on the table for him. Not as a fair fight, but as a sacrifice. The crowds at these fights are getting more and more bloodthirsty. Prentice could probably make a small fortune out of a one-sided bloodbath, to seal the reputation of one of his young guns.'

'But...'

'But nothing, Ree. Prentice is one horrible, ruthless bastard. Your dad doesn't know his arse from his elbow at the moment, and Prentice is likely to offer him a lump of cash he can't refuse. For one last go.'

Tears welled-up in Rita's eyes; she turned them on H in desperation.

'What are we going to do H? What are we going to do?'

'There's only one thing we can do – I'll have to straighten Lennie Prentice out, get him to back off.'

'How on earth are you going to do that? He's ruthless, he's a major figure, he's got a small army of minders round him at all times H, it's him who straightens people out, not the other way round. Think it through.'

'I have Ree, listen darling. It's Prentice or your dad, by the look of it. Don't worry, I won't go in half-cocked. And I'll take Chuck with me. He might be drunk as ten men now, but he's as good as ten men when you've got a serious job of work to get done.'

***

Chuck had a lie-in the following morning. H killed two birds with one stone by arranging to have a drink with his old mate Ronnie Ruddock – he could have a hair of the dog and pick Ronnie's brains about Prentice, with whom he'd had dealings. Ronnie, H was learning on this trip, seemed to have dealings with everyone. They met at midday in the George Inn at the Borough.

'How's it going then, Ron?' said H, once they'd established themselves in one of the pub's many nooks and crannies. 'You're looking good. That overcoat must've come to a nice few quid on its own.'

'Clothes maketh the man H. I have to turn myself out properly these days, mate. Got to look the part.'

'So what are you doing?'

'I'm just getting into futures and options. I'm working for a firm just across the river from here.'

'What's an option?'

'It's like an each-way bet on the gee-gees. You buy the right to buy shares or sell shares at a certain price. If the markets move in your favour you can buy them or sell them, even though you never owned them.'

'Sounds complicated.'

'No, it's simple,' said Ronnie, warming to his subject, 'and a future is like an option with a few technical differences. What you have to understand...'

H tried to understand but the world of high finance was not his thing and he changed the subject.

'Didn't realise you had the qualifications for that sort of thing Ron.'

'You don't need qualifications to get in front in the City these days, mate. These days, if you've got plenty of front, and good instincts, and you're double-shrewd round a pound note, you can get your foot in the door. And get to where the money is.'

'Fuck me, you've come a long way fast. Caked-up with money then, are you?'

'Not really, mate, not yet. But I will be. I had a long hard look at myself when I left the army, when I was recovering from my injury...I decided life is short, and that I was going to aim for the top.'

'So you're not running a stall down East Lane anymore?' said H with a grin.

'No, not anymore. I never did really – I got more into selling insurance to the stallholders in the end. Less work, more money. That's how I got started.'

'What can you tell me about Lenny Prentice? I'm interested in his set up.'

'What's your interest in Prentice?'

'I'll tell you later.'

'OK...like I said, I sold insurance policies to a lot of stallholders – well, most of them actually, in the end. He owns a couple of stalls, one sells jewellery and the other sells kids' toys. Took me ages to find out he was the real owner.'

'Why?'

'He runs them under limited companies and those themselves are part of an umbrella company. I had to research at Companies House before I figured it all out.'

'He's a bit sharp then?'

'Yeah. Very, very shrewd, and ruthless.'

'Is he still in The Blue?'

'Yep, he's got offices there, in the market. Above the baker's. It's where he runs everything from. He's extended the range of his operations. Big time. It's not just the stalls and the fight promotion. He owns pawn shops, burger stalls, taxi firms, security firms, and I should think he probably does a fair bit of protection and drug wholesaling as well – at a safe distance. He's into everything, basically. Now he is caked-up.'

'I suppose he dishes out plenty of violence when necessary, to keep things ticking over nicely?'

'Yep, he's famous for it. Never gets his own hands dirty, of course. But he employs top-notch muscle, and from what I hear he's an absolute fucking bully. Never one to take no for an answer.'

'You still have dealings with him?'

47

'Yep, from time to time. He wants to get into riverside property, you know, warehouse conversions and all that. So do I. That's the coming thing – a lot of the old places we used to muck about in in Rotherhithe when we was kids will be worth an absolute fortune soon. So we move in some of the same circles.'

'Can you get me a meeting with him?'

'What…?'

'A meeting Ron. It's a simple question: can you get me a meeting?'

'Why on God's green earth do you want a meeting with Lennie Prentice?'

'I just want to talk to him, man to man. Can you get me in there with him or not?'

'Well, I'd like to know what your thinking is mate. I've put a fair bit into building my relationship with him, and various others.'

'My thinking, Ron, is to ask him nicely to stop taking advantage of someone close to me. If he won't listen to reason, I plan to slap him and his famous minders all the way up and down Southwark Park Road until he agrees to cease and desist.'

At this Ronnie laughed out loud. 'You and whose army?' he said.

'The US Army, mate. I'm talking about Delta Force back up. I'm going to bring Lenny fucking Prentice down a peg or two.'

'You can't be serious, mate. You really want me to set it up so you can put it on him in his own place? It'll never work, he's properly protected at all times – plus it'll wreck everything I'm putting together if people think I'm capable of setting something like that up. I'd do anything for you H, if it really came to it. You know that. But this doesn't even make sense. Think of another way.'

H and Prentice had crossed paths plenty of times over the years, as faces do. They'd been in the same pubs, passed the odd hello. But they'd never had a full conversation. H had never liked loudmouthed bullies, and Prentice was about ten years his senior, so he'd never sought him out.

'You better wait here Chuck.' said H as he pulled up and parked round the back of The Blue the next morning. 'I just want to put a marker down, let him know I'm on him. Nothing's going to happen.'

'No, I'm coming in with you.'

The two young men held each other's stare. H had given Chuck the option to back out. But Chuck Vaughan was about as likely to back out of a situation as Harry Hawkins was. H smiled. 'OK, but hang back, behind me a bit, yeah?' he said as he jumped out the car and headed for the office entrance, which was accessed by a side door in a narrow alleyway. The entrance had a snazzy new entry system. H hit the bell and the speaker system sprang into life.

'Yes?'

'Harry Hawkins, to see Lennie.'

H pushed the door open at the sound of the buzzer. He and Chuck swarmed up the rickety wooden staircase and were met at the top by four pumped-up minders who looked like they'd come from the Mr. Universe muscle man contest. H heard Chuck snigger behind him; he said nothing, but just looked the leading minder in the eye.

'Wait here,' said minder one. He returned a full ten minutes later to find H in agitated mood, working his jaw hard and pacing up and down between Chuck and his three colleagues.

'He'll see you now.'

'Come on Chuck,' said H.

'No. Just you.'

The words prompted minders two, three and four to block the path of Chuck, who sniggered again and stood easy with his hands in his pockets – he'd assumed the stance of a man completely sure of himself, and unimpressed by his potential adversaries. H could sense his friend beginning to get the flavour. But H had come to parley, to negotiate in the first instance in a spirit of reasonableness. He put his hand up to pacify the American.

'It's OK. Give me five minutes. Don't do anything nasty to these boys while I'm gone.'

H followed minder one along a dirty corridor, into an open-plan office decorated, if that was the word, with peeling white paint and a stained brown carpet. They crossed to a door in the corner and minder one knocked twice.

'Come in.'

The minder opened the door and stood aside for H. The office was as dilapidated as the rest of the building, and sparsely furnished: one plain drinks table containing bottles of scotch, vodka and mixers; one padlocked filing cabinet; one beat-up old desk supporting one phone, one jotting pad, one address book and one ostentatiously displayed pistol. The only luxurious feature was the large leather office chair Prentice sat in, smiling, relaxed and reclining with his hands clasped behind his back like he didn't have a care in the world.

'Young Hawkins,' said Prentice, asserting his seniority.

'Mr. Prentice…I must say I didn't expect to find a man with your reputation plotted up in a pisshole like this.' Prentice was visibly irked by this – he hadn't expected such confidence and immediate aggression from a nobody he remembered as being not much more than a kid.

'Whatever,' he said. 'You've got five minutes. I agreed to see you out of respect to your father – if it wasn't for that you wouldn't be here, so you can leave all the bollocks out. What do you want?'

'I want to talk to you about Jimmy Jefferson.'

'What about him?'

'I'm here on behalf of his Rita to ask you to stop promoting him. His brains are fucked now, as you of all people must know, and he's not capable of making decisions in his own best interest. Rita is seeing a lawyer about taking legal control of his affairs pending an assessment. In the meantime, I'm here to inform you that he's retiring from the game, effective as of now.'

'I don't think so.'

'I do. He's too old. It's too risky.'

'He's a legend. Always gives a hundred and ten percent. The punters love him. If he wants to fight, he fights.'

'Not anymore.'

'Well, let's not be hasty. If I lose a fighter I need a replacement. You look like you can handle yourself. Now, if you're willing to step up...'

'No way. It's a fucking mugs game.'

'So your friend's a mug?'

'No, you're mugging him. And I'm asking you nicely to stop.'

'That's not how it works, sunshine.'

'Listen clever bollocks, I'm fucking warning you, lay off him.'

'Warning me? You're fucking warning me?'

Prentice addressed his next comment to the minder: 'Right then. Young Mr Hawkins is leaving now. His five minutes are up. Please escort him out.' He turned his gaze towards H: 'You, my son, can piss right off and never darken my fucking doorstep again.'

H's options flashed through his mind in an instant. He wasn't scared, and he had Chuck Vaughan outside waiting to back him up. Part of him, a big part, wanted to take Lennie Prentice by the scruff of the neck and put his head straight through the window. But he held himself in check – this was not the time or place. And there was the hand gun to consider. He gave Prentice the look of death and walked out without another word.

'How'd it go?' said Chuck, twisting his large frame down the narrow staircase.

'Badly – the geezer's an absolute cunt, but he's well-organised. We'll have to bide our time for a bit and box clever if we're going to get at him,' said H as they made their way back to the car.

***

One Thursday in late November H, back in Belfast, received a troubling call from Rita; her dad was back on his feet, and had been persuaded by Prentice to put his hands up, just as H had predicted, for one last bout and a massive payday. He still hadn't had his brain looked at, said Rita, but his mental state had worsened and some days he barely knew what he was saying or doing. But his physical recovery had gone well, and Prentice had Jimmy 'The Rottweiler' Jefferson v. Johnny 'The Gypsy Assassin' Mahoney lined up for December 20th in an as-yet undisclosed venue near Dartford. It was the fight of the year.

In the days after the call H begged and pleaded for a forty-eight-hour compassionate leave pass until he got it, and was back in Bermondsey at his parent's flat by Saturday morning. H, his parents and brother Tony, who'd turned into a strapping twenty-two-year-old man with boxing ambitions of his own, were joined by Rita, Chuck Vaughan on compassionate leave of his own, synchronised with H's, and a couple of his dad's friends – Tiny Abbott and Mickey Casey – around the kitchen table. They were keeping this in-house; the area was filled these days with Prentice people, active supporters and beneficiaries of his business acumen alike. The head of the family chaired the meeting.

'What exactly are you proposing, H?'

'We have to stop this fight, pop, or Jimmy Jefferson will wind up in a hospital bed sucking up his dinner through a straw. Have you seen this fucking Mahoney? He's terrifying, he would probably have destroyed The Rottweiler even at his peak.'

'Yes, yes, I've got all that, H. But what are you proposing? Why are we all here?'

'We have to put it on Prentice, I mean really put it on him. I've been and had a word with him already.'

'So I understand. You've got some front son, I'll give you that. What did he say?'

'He fucked me off after thirty seconds.'

'Sounds pretty final, H. Not much you can do after that, is there?'

'Not unless we take it up a notch, no.'

'Meaning?'

'Meaning we put it on him...challenge his authority.'

'Listen son, you've always been a brave and impetuous little sod. A bit like your old man here, but you can't go around threatening the likes of Lennie Prentice and expect them to just back down. The harder you try and push him, the harder he'll come back at you.'

'He's a fucking wanker. I can take him.'

'Maybe so, but a wanker with a shedload of money and an army of bodyguards.'

'We just let the fight go ahead then?'

'Jimmy's a grown man. He's agreed to it.'

'No, please,' said Rita, 'we've got to stop the fight; this one will destroy him, I know it will.'

'Listen, pop,' said H,' let's say you're right and we can't get at him the old-school way. Is there anything else we can try, other options?'

'Well, trying to talk sense to Jimmy is out – right out; I've been on at him for days. He won't back down. He's always been stubborn – even more stubborn than you are. And that was before his brains got fucked. As far as Jimmy's concerned the fight is on. He's looking forward to it.'

'Maybe, just this once,' said H's mum Eileen, 'we can let the police know what's happening?'

The collective groan that rose up around the table said that this was not an option; that this was never an option.

'Nah, mum,' said Tony, 'we've got to handle this ourselves – not that it looks like there's much we can do, except try to capture Prentice and batter the fuck out of him.'

'You better be ready for the comeback son, if you want to go down that road,' said his dad. 'Prentice is completely ruthless, he's got no scruples at all. He'd come for all of us. Me, you, your mother, H, the others. No, son, you can't just bash him up. You'd have to kill him. Stone fucking dead. And you'd have to be sure no one knew it was you. People round here have only just stopped talking about the last little courtesy visit H paid him.'

The room went quiet. The Hawkins family and associates had never been averse to a bit of ducking and diving around the edges of the law, and they could always hold their own when it came to a little street-level toe-to-toe... but murder? H had never heard his dad talk like this.

'Kill him? Fucking hell, pop.'

'You can either top him, H, or you can leave the whole thing be. Them's your options.'

H sat down, deflated. He had no words in response to his father's advice. His eyes turned to Rita. He loved her like a sister, and would do almost anything for her. But murdering someone for talking a fighter into a fight, that fell outside H's definition of 'almost anything.' The party drank the rest of the weekend away in the Rayfield Arms, and H headed back to Belfast on the Sunday evening with a sore head, and an even sorer heart.

# February 1985

H couldn't get back to London again until well after Christmas, well after the Jefferson v. Mahoney fight. But he knew how that had gone. He headed straight from Paddington station to the Walworth Road at the start of his week's leave. He knocked at the Jefferson's door and nearly fell through the floor when Rita answered it. She looked ten years older than she had in November: her hair had strands of grey in it, she'd put on a fair bit of weight, and her eyes were so puffy they looked as if the Gypsy Assassin had walloped her around the ring, on top of crippling her dad.

The spark had gone out of her. H watched her closely as she shuffled slowly around the kitchen making tea – the slow, deliberate movements, the immobile, expressionless face and the numb-sounding, rote answers to his questions told him that she was now adrift in the deep depression/heavy medication vortex.

'So how is he, Ree?'

'"Severely mentally impaired", they call it. He can hardly talk, though he seems to know what's going on around him sometimes, his eyes are open and all that. Crippled from the waist down. Spinal column – he'll never walk again. He's as miserable as sin…he's asked me to top him off a couple of times already.'

'How long they going to keep him in hospital for?'

'Don't know yet. They're working with social services on his assessment and getting the equipment I'll need here to look after him. Then I can become his official carer. I've already turned my job in, so…'

She trailed off and, sitting at the table with both hands wrapped around her mug, threw a thousand yard stare out of the window. The Guy's hospital tower was visible, H noticed. She must spend a lot of time looking at it. This is what her world had shrunk to: the never-ending visits to the hospital on the number 35 bus, on the days when she was up to it; the daily fistful of pills to numb the pain in her soul; the endless cups of tea in the kitchen, in her ragged grey dressing gown and carpet slippers; the view from the window.

*\*\*\**

'It's in Beckenham,' said Chuck, back at H's parents after three days surveillance duty, 'a big detached house. It's huge, with a big iron gate at the front and high walls at the sides. He's safety conscious, that's for sure. He doesn't get out of the car until the gate is closed.'

'Minders?'

'Three. The driver and two others. They look about outside every now and then. No pattern.'

'Are these three always in the picture? Do they sleep at the house?'

'Not all of them, no – but there's at least always one, far as I can tell.'

'No one else. Apart from the guards I think he lives alone.'

'Confirms what my old man told me,' said H, 'that he's divorced, and his two kids live with his ex-wife.' What are the security arrangements?'

'He's got a chickenshit camera system, up on the gate and the outside of the house – these guys always think that's going to help them, for some reason. The gate itself is crap; it looks impressive but a child of ten could go through it if he knew what he was doing. And there's a little old Alsatian out front. This guy Prentice is all hat and no cattle.'

'So you can deal with that lot?' said H.

'Can a bear shit in the woods? Come on buddy, can't you find me something hard to do?'

'How about taking care of the minders?'

Chuck Vaughan laughed out loud, slapped his thigh and said 'Sheeeit, Harry. I hope you're fixin' to give me something to get my teeth into while I'm here. This is sure as hell ain't it.'

'Alright, John Wayne, slow down. You say there's not much of a pattern to his movements?'

'Not over the three days I've watched him. But he's never got home later than midnight. Not much of a night-owl, I'd say. Needs his beauty sleep.'

'So we set the stake out up for nine, to be on the safe side. I want to be sure we see him going in.'

'Yep,' said Chuck. 'And I'd say we go in either tonight or tomorrow, if you want me to deal with his ladies-in-waiting. I got to get back.'

'OK then, there's no time like the present. Let's have a bit of dinner and get down there tonight.'

'Sure, buddy…as long as you don't take me to no more of your goddam "Wimpy" bars – what kind of a place is that for a man to eat in, anyway? I need a steak, Harry. Get me a good steak before we head out and I'll have those boys trussed up like hogs on a spit before you even break into a sweat with ol' Lennie.'

*** 

They pulled up and parked three hundred yards short of Prentice's place at nine-fifteen. Chuck knew Prentice's Bentley by sight – all they had to do was hunker down in H's car and wait. H sat in the back, low down, to minimise the chance of anyone spotting him, while Chuck sat in the front seat and fiddled with the radio, scanning the airwaves for music he could sing along to. But of country music there was none, and after ten minutes of frustration he switched the radio off and treated H to his own renditions of his favourite Waylon Jennings and Bob Wills songs. H enjoyed this well enough up to a point – Chuck was a spirited and tuneful performer – but half an hour in it began to wear a little thin.

He requested a change of programme, looking at his watch as he did so. It was nine forty-five, and Chuck was beginning to warm to his new theme – a loquacious recommendation of Texan women – when he broke off and said 'OK H, game on. Here they come in the old rear-view.'

Prentice's car cruised slowly past them, and fifty yards out from the house the big gates slid open. The driver eased the car in and onto the small driveway, and H and Chuck waited until all four car doors had been slammed shut before talking things through one last time.

Chuck pulled on a black balaclava, zipped up his jacket, got out of the car and went back to pop the boot and retrieve his work bag. He was going old-school: a little jammer-gizmo for the cameras, grappling hook and rope for the side wall, small tranquiliser-dart pistol for the dog, should he need it, chloroform and duct tape for Prentice's men, and a pistol with a long black silencer to do the persuading. Experience had taught him that if you point a silenced weapon at a man late at night he assumes you're going to shoot him, and is likely to become grateful and compliant when you don't, but start issuing orders instead.

'Give me twenty, H, then come out back to the garden – I'll have your boy ready and waiting.'

H got out of the car after fifteen minutes, and walked towards the front of the gate just in time to hear it sliding open. He continued on up the driveway and round to the back in silence. He passed a garage on his way; all was still quiet, but when he peeked into its window he saw two men, trussed-up and unconscious. There was no sign of the dog, but he had enough trust in Chuck's capabilities to keep moving, and after a few moments more he turned into the garden itself and saw another man trussed-up and out for the count, the dog sitting quietly at Chuck's feet, and Prentice himself, kneeling with his hands on his head on the wet grass. Chuck was training his silenced weapon straight at Prentice's forehead.

'Alrighty, H,' said Chuck. 'Here's your boy – I'll leave you to it. I'm going into the house for some of that fine brandy; swing by and get me when you're done.' He turned and ambled slowly towards the house with the dog trailing after him.

'Alright, Prentice, on your feet. It's show time – time for a nice little straightener: Big Lenny Prentice v. Little Harry Hawkins. Bare-knuckle rules apply.'

'Listen, son,' said Prentice, struggling to his feet, 'there's no need for all this. There's a safe in the house with more money in it than I know what to do with. Come in with me...we'll have a nice little drink with your American mate, and talk terms. I reckon...'

'Not interested,' said H through gritted teeth. 'You weren't interested in whether or not Jimmy Jefferson lived or died, and I'm not interested in how you come out of this. Put your hands up.'

Prentice swallowed hard, and did what he was told. But it was years since he'd fought in earnest, or got his own hands dirty – he was out of practice, and out of shape. H advanced on him without another word and aimed an uppercut at his jaw. He dodged it, but not the next one, which came before he'd steadied himself. It knocked him onto his back. H leant down and picked him up, gripping the cloth of his Jermyn Street shirt for purchase.

Prentice stood, already unsteady on his feet, while H rained rapid-fire blows to his abdomen and the side of his head. Again he went down, and again H pulled him up.

'Fight me, you bastard,' said H, jogging on the spot. 'Come on. I thought you liked fighting...fight me.'

Prentice, now angry and finally engaged, lunged at H and was once again put down; the younger man was just too fast, too strong, too ruthless – a young lion in his prime. Prentice understood, with horror, that H was as ruthless a fighting machine as the young guns he was promoting. He let himself fall one more time, and rolled over onto his back.

'Get up,' said H.

'No.'

'Don't make me ask you again.'

'No, I'm staying here.'

H got down low, spun Prentice over onto his belly, and aimed kick after kick into the small of his back until he begged for mercy.

'OK...OK then,' said H, standing up and breathing hard. 'That's for Jimmy Jefferson, and all the other poor bastards you've ruined.' Prentice said nothing, but stayed where he was, trying to process the pain.

'OK, listen now, Prentice,' said H, glaring down at him. 'And listen hard. You've got a lot at stake here, and I want the situation to be clear, OK? Listening?'

Prentice looked at H but showed no emotion.

'Can you hear me Len? I hope that blood I see trickling out of your ear's not impairing your hearing. Nod once if you can hear me, son.'

Prentice nodded.

'Right – you will recall that some time ago I asked you nicely to do me and Rita Jefferson a little favour, but you wouldn't have it. Jimmy Jefferson's halfway to being a vegetable now, and he'll never walk again. That's on you, one hundred percent on you. I've come back to clarify the situation and set matters straight. That's on you as well.'

A look of impotent rage came into Prentice's eyes, as far as H could tell in the gloom, but still he said nothing.

'So as far as I'm concerned we're all square now. Now, I do understand that in your world all this requires a response. But think hard, Len, think it through; if one hair on one head of someone close to me is harmed I'll be back, and I'll blow your whole fucking world up before you've even had a chance to watch it happen. I'll have people with me who know how to do that. I'm not talking about the sort of monkeys you employ, son – all your fucking superannuated football hooligans and pumped-up gym bunnies. No, I'm talking about Paratroopers, and SAS and Delta Force men. I'm talking about coming after you ten-handed with world class, fully equipped and trained and experienced killers and wreckers.'

He looked down at the frozen form of Prentice, who was now shivering with cold, or something worse, and let his message sink in.

'Alright then son? Have I made myself clear?'

Prentice nodded.

'Right then, I think we understand each other at last. I'm going to put you to sleep now. Chew carefully over what's happened here when you wake up.'

Prentice tried to rise up to make some sort of statement, but it was too late; he couldn't move, and H was already in motion. The last thing he saw before the lights went out was H's heel moving down towards his head, and the last thing he heard was 'One hair, on one head.'

# On Tour

# 1978 – Thursday

'Where the fuck is Shy Nervous John?' said H.

'I think he's in the khazi. He went a bit strong on these beers. I warned him about going mental on the boat, but you know him, he can't help himself,' said Ronnie.

'Looks like he's not the only one. I…'

Once again, the gigantic ferry was thrown up clear of the water by some massive unseen wave, and spent what seemed like an age suspended, for all its bulk, high in the air.

H counted it down: '1,2,3…'

Boom. The vessel crashed back down into the water with sickening force, shaking the structure of the boat, the fixtures and fittings inside it, and the internal organs of its passengers. It was three o'clock in the morning, and the Hook of Holland seemed a long way off.

'How much longer we got on this fucking thing, Ron?'

'Four, four and half hours.'

H groaned and spread himself out across two of the bar's upright chairs, and prayed for sleep. It didn't come. He opened his eyes and watched a stream of human body fluids roll down from the toilet area and into the bar as the ferry lurched sharply to one side.

'Fuck this for a game of soldiers,' he said, 'I'm going up on deck to look for the others.'

\*\*\*

H found Billy Marshall and Chris 'The Scaffold' Casey holding onto the ship's rail for dear life, howling into the wind and daring the North Sea to take them. H, being the team captain and senior player in the party at a full nineteen years old, had been asked to keep an eye on these two by Billy's mother – it was the first time her seventeen-year-old and his mate had been away from home for any length of time. H knew the pair of them were a handful and hadn't really wanted to bring them, but Billy was the best centre forward he'd played with and they would need a proven goal scorer if they were to have any chance against the teams they would face in Amsterdam and Hamburg.

Anglers Athletic under-21s were on tour. H didn't have high hopes of success on the pitch, but the prospect of nearly a week's worth of fun and games off it in two of the tastiest spots in Europe was too good to pass up – he, Ronnie Ruddock and Shy Nervous John Viney were going to cut loose, and have the time of their lives.

'Alright boys?' said H. 'How's it going?'

'Not all that, mate,' said The Scaffold. 'We was feeling a bit Pat and Mick, so we came up for a bit of air. Too much scotch, I think.'

'Fuck me Scaff,' said H, 'the barman served you scotch? You only look about twelve. Is this what you call training? These Dutchmen will run rings round us if you lot are all in bits with hangovers.'

The Scaffold said nothing, but turned sharply towards the open sea again, there to disgorge once again the contents of his stomach, such as they were.

'They're going to fucking run rings round us anyway H,' said Billy, laughing uproariously at his friend's misfortune. 'Total Football and all that.'

Total Football, a tactical theory of the game that meant any outfield player could take over the role of any other player, had been made famous by the Dutch – although the British still preferred less flexible systems.

'We'll be alright if we get in amongst them with a few crunching tackles early on. These Europeans don't like it up 'em,' said H. 'That's if any of youse lot are sober enough to know what the fuck's going on.'

65

'Well, I dunno,' said Billy. 'Anyway, the barman didn't serve us the scotch. Pickett got them for us.'

'Pickett? Tony fucking Pickett? Some sort of leader he's turning out to be. Where is he now?'

'I thought you was in charge H,' said Billy.

'Well, I am really, but they said we had to have a proper looking grown-up manager to front the tour. Someone over twenty-one. Where's the fat idiot now?'

'Last we saw of him he was heading for that observation deck upstairs. He was absolutely paralytic, as drunk as ten men, you'll probably find him smashed out of his head up there.'

\*\*\*

They – H, Ronnie and a badly hungover Shy Nervous John – caught sight of the Hook of Holland at seven o'clock. The bar area in which they'd passed most of the night looked like the IRA had been at it. Bodies strewn around on the chairs, tables and floor, upturned and damaged looking furniture scattered here and there, rivulets and puddles of booze and human effluence everywhere, and a stink like the Black Hole of Calcutta.

'Jesus wept,' said Ronnie, 'have a look at the state of this lot. Thank fuck we've arrived.'

'Yeah, long night mate,' said H. 'Still, it's Friday, and we'll be in Amsterdam in a couple of hours. Bit of kip at the hostel and then out on the town mate, all-systems-go.'

'Yes mate,' said Ronnie, 'all-systems-fucking-go. Them brasses in the windows won't know what's hit 'em when I turn up.'

'Easy tiger, all in good time,' said H. 'Right, I'll go and see if I can root Pickett out – we'll need him to get through passport control. You have a go at rousing Shy Nervous John.'

'Why d'you lot always call him that? Shy Nervous John?' asked Billy Marshall, rearing up out of nowhere, full of beans.

'That's his name,' said H.

'No, but you always call him "Shy Nervous John", never just "John", or "Shy Nervous" or something. Seems like a right mouthful.'

'Yeah, it is a bit of an effort, keeping it up all the time,' said Ronnie.

'Why do it then?' said Billy.

'Because he hates it,' said H.

# Friday

H regained consciousness on his bunk at three o'clock. Bright autumn sunshine flowed in through the window. Ronnie and Shy Nervous John were snoring loudly, but there was no one else to be seen. Pickett, and Billy, The Scaffold and the rest of the players had already made themselves scarce. H shuddered at the thought of what they would already be up to, and a nightmarish vision of the following day's game flashed across his mind. He dismissed it and moved straight onto more important things.

'Alright ladies,' he shouted at Ronnie and Shy Nervous John, 'rise and shine. We can't lay about here all day. We've got beer to drink, drugs to take, prostitutes to get hold of.'

The hostel was right at the centre of things, just off the Damrak. They made themselves presentable as quickly as they could and surged up to Dam Square on foot in a state of high excitement, without talking, their senses taking in the sights, sounds, smells of a new place. None of them had ever been out of England before.

'Right,' said H when they reached the square, 'let's plot up here for a minute and work up a plan.'

'There's no need for all that H,' said Ronnie. 'You want to get into the beer, so let's do that first. Shy Nervous John wants to get into the weed or whatever, so we can have a dabble at that after. I want to get hold of a brass, so let's go to the red-light district a bit later, when it gets dark and livens up.'

His two friends nodded their assent.

'Right,' said H, 'let's have a few beers then. What's the name of the bar Pickett recommended? He might know fuck-all about football, or much of anything else, but he does know his way around a pint.'

'It's called the Cary's Bar, it's just around the corner; here, on Spuistraat,' said Ronnie, pointing at his map.

'Right, let's have it,' said Shy Nervous John, 'let's fucking have it.'

Ronnie marched them through side streets back in the direction they'd come for ten minutes, until they came upon what they were looking for: an unremarkable looking Brown Bar sandwiched between sex shops.

The inside was gloomy and inviting, like an English pub, and already lively with hardened looking drinkers, most of them Irishmen or Brits. H barrelled up to the bar and ordered beers while his friends found a table. The barman produced three tiny glasses not amounting to much more than glorified egg cups, pumped them to overflowing with yellow foam, wiped the foam away with a wooden spatula type thing that looked like the kind of instrument doctors shove down their patient's throats before asking them to say 'aagh', and presented them to H about half-full of actual beer. He laughed out loud at the sight of them.

'I asked for beers mate. What are these?' he said in good humour.

'Beers,' said the barman in flawless sarcastic English. 'Dutch beers. You want them or not?'

H paid up and got them to the table in one piece.

'What the fuck are these?' said Ronnie.

'That wanker of a barman called them "beers",' said H.

'There's fuck-all beer in these things mate,' said Shy Nervous John, taking a slug, 'and it's as weak as piss. We're going to struggle to get anywhere with these.'

'Then you'd better go and get another round in, hadn't you son,' said H, 'so we can get cracking.'

H leaned back in his chair and took in the surroundings through the thick pub fug: the grizzled looking hedonists gearing up for Friday night, the sticky carpet and rickety wooden furniture, the fraying dartboard – it all looked comfortably familiar. He scanned the framed pictures on the walls and saw old paintings of figures skating on snowbound canals, footballers, actors and celebrities he didn't recognise, the front pages of newspapers carrying pictures, mostly, of historic events.

The Dubliners' *Dirty Old Town* blared through the speakers. Shy Nervous John was still at the bar, taking his time getting served. H sighed, rolled his eyes at Ronnie and got up to have a look at the framed newspapers. He was surprised to find they were mostly British, and nearly all tabloids.

Suddenly the relative calm of the bar was shattered by a blood curdling shout of 'What the fuck is all this?'

H turned to face the room with what Ronnie knew, with a sinking feeling, was his ready-for-it stance.

'Have a look at this Ron. They've got half a dozen papers here with front page news of the IRA blowing up Lord Mountbatten. What is this, some sort of IRA gaff?' he shouted to no one in particular. He ain't even fucking cold in his grave yet.'

Receiving no answer, H turned his attention once again to the pictures, clawing the frames from the wall like a man possessed. He turned to the room. 'I'm not fucking having this.'

He headed for the bar, or rather for the barman, to have it out with him, when he felt a hand land firmly on his left shoulder, and then another on his right. 'Leave it mate, it ain't worth it,' said Ronnie.

By this H was pulled up short. He returned to his senses, and saw that he'd been on the verge of running amok. He stepped back from the bar, into open space, with his friends either side of him, staying close. From his right side Shy Nervous John whispered into his ear, as an air of Mexican standoff prevailed:

70

'Mate, think it through. We're in a different country, they do things different. And we've come here for a laugh. If you go off now, we'll all finish up getting nicked. Come on mate, we've only been in Amsterdam for five minutes.'

H relaxed his shoulders, and looked his friend in the eye, nodding.

'Top man. You know it makes sense. Let's go and get hold of some weed somewhere, that'll calm us down. The beer's shit anyway.'

***

'Right boys,' said Shy Nervous John as they made their way back towards the square, 'what we need to find is a good coffeeshop.'

'Fuck that,' said H, 'who wants coffee? I want to get into the beers, or whatever else they got here that passes for booze.'

'No mate, I'm talking about a cannabis place – they just call them coffeeshops here. You buy your gear, you buy a coffee, and Bob's your uncle.'

'Fair enough. Where to then, Gunga Din?'

'Well, there's a well-known one called the Bulldog.'

'Where is it?'

'How the fuck do I know? Let's just jump in a cab.'

'No need for that mate,' said Ronnie, 'it's just around the corner from here. I can't pronounce the street, but here it is on the map, look.'

'How'd you know it's there?' said H.

'Because I did my research mate. Jesus, what is it with you people?'

***

H and Ronnie sank into their low soft chairs and took in the ambience. Shy Nervous John did the business at the bar, came back to their table and got cracking with the rizla papers. The smell of weed and hash – H had no idea what the difference was, so the others enlightened him – was overpowering.

'What's that tune?' said H.

'Steve Miller Band, mate,' said Shy Nervous John 'The Joker. I was hoping they'd have something more up to date, less hippy-ish.'

'Like what?' said Ronnie.

'I dunno, The Fall, or at least The Clash or something. Something with a bit of bite. It's like nineteen-seventy-five in 'ere.'

'I thought you were here to get nice and relaxed,' said H.

'I'm here to get well charged up mate, and take it from there. Here, get your laughing gear round this,' said Shy Nervous John, passing H the finished joint he'd been lovingly preparing.

H, who had only ever smoked once before at a party and had not particularly enjoyed the experience, took it, took a puff and sat back waiting for something to happen. He closed his eyes and listened to the music for a minute or two, feeling relaxed at first but then edgy, twitchy, unsure of why he was here or where here was. He opened his eyes to see the other two giggling like schoolgirls and pointing. At him.

'What's the matter H,' said Ronnie,' you struggling mate?'

'What d'you mean, struggling? Why would I be struggling?'

'You look like you might be getting a bit paranoid mate – like the gear's getting into your nut.' said Shy Nervous John.

'No. No paranoia here – I leave all that to you. That's your fucking job mate, being shy and nervous and paranoid.'

'Easy H, easy,' said Ronnie. 'Slow down mate. No need to be like that. Shy Nervous John's got enough on his plate without you digging him out. Ready for more then?'

'No, I fucking am not. I'm starting to think all this is not really my cup of tea.'

'Want to go somewhere else?' asked Ronnie.

'Yep, I think I do. Somewhere they got beer. I'm gagging for a pint.'

'Paradiso,' said Shy Nervous John, 'they got all the booze, drugs and music we could want there, there'll probably be a few sorts knocking about as well. And if you don't manage to pull, Ron, we can just march onto the red light after.'

'Sweet,' said Ronnie. 'Sweet as a fucking nut. Let's go.'

\*\*\*

'Ah, that's more like it,' said H, after downing a cold, full-sized Heineken from a proper glass. Ronnie raised his in agreement, and smiled. 'Yep, a few more of these and we'll be ready to rock and roll. What d'you want to do, H, give it another hour or so and get down to the red light? I can't have a lot more of this music – I'll wind up with a migraine.'

The bar of Amsterdam's Paradiso, on a beautiful autumn night, with decent beer and prostitutes in windows to come later. Life could be worse, and H and Ronnie were finally getting into the groove.

'Yep, when Shy Nervous John's finished mooching about looking for more drugs or whatever it is he's doing we'll collar him and put him in the picture,' said H.

'Well he can stay here and get drugged up and listen to this shit all night mate as far as I'm concerned – what does he call it, "post-punk"? Not exactly Mickey Jack, is it? *Off the Wall*, now that's an album you can listen to all the fucking way through. I don't know how you stand it round his gaff, listening to all that bollocks all the time.'

73

'I like some of it. Some of the stuff he comes up with is horrible, I'll give you that. But he's got some blinding stuff as well. Anyway, get the beers in mate, I'm gasping.'

'Oi Oi!' said Ronnie. 'Speak of the devil, here's the man himself. Fancy a nice cold Heineken, Shy Nervous John?'

'Nah, I'll have an orange juice or something Ron. Something soft.'

'Any joy mate, find what you were looking for?' said H.

'Yep, I certainly fucking did,' said Shy Nervous John, turning his hand over with a huge grin and opening his fist to reveal what looked like three tiny squares of paper. 'Acid blotters mate, the best in Amsterdam, the geezer reckons. He says this gear will absolutely blow our socks off.'

'Well, I'm going to stick with the beers for now mate,' said H. 'I'll see how you and Ronnie get on with it and jump in later if it's shaping up alright.'

'You bailing out on me? What you scared of, you fucking tart? Big Harry Hawkins, scared of a little bit of acid...I thought we was all in this together?'

'I make H right,' said Ronnie. 'A bit of puff is one thing, but I've heard that gear can make you go off your head. No need to get stroppy mate, each to his own. Listen, I want to have my wits about me when we get to the red light – I don't want to get into one of them birds in the windows and start dribbling all over her like a spastic. H is right mate, you lead the way and we'll catch up with you a bit later. Anyway, this way we can keep our eye on you.'

'Tarts. Absolute fucking tarts, the pair of you. Well, here's to Ian Curtis,' said Shy Nervous John, throwing the three blotters down his neck with a flourish and gulping them down. 'If you want to catch up with me later you'll have to sort your own gear out.'

\*\*\*

Shy Nervous John melted into the crowd, there to commune with the music and the universe at large. H stayed at the bar, giving the Heineken pump a hammering. Ronnie stayed with him for a bit, then went on walkabout to see what he could see. He returned half hour later, flushed and happy.

'There's another room upstairs mate,' he said. 'It's more like a club, they're playing proper music – there's a DJ from London up there, we've had Cheryl Lynn, McFadden and Whitehead, Narada Michael Walden…Let's find silly bollocks and get up there for a boogie. There's a few sorts up there and all.'

'Alright mate, let me just finish this one.'

'Any idea where he is? You been keeping an eye on him?'

'Well…' said H.

'Alright, you finish your beer and I'll go and round him up.'

***

He was nowhere to be found. Ronnie took a long, slow turn around the entire place, peering hard into all the darkened corners, and came back empty handed.

'We'll have to double up H. I've looked everywhere – here, upstairs, downstairs, outside, there's no sign of him anywhere.'

'You looked in the khazi?' said H, suddenly remembering that Shy Nervous John had lately developed a habit of heading to those when things got a bit much for him.

'Yeah, I went in there…nothing. Can't say I liked the look of it in there much though. Things looked like they might be getting a bit lively, one way or another,' said Ronnie.

'I reckon it's worth another look,' said H. 'I'll wager he's pugged himself away in there.'

'Alright, follow me then,' said Ronnie, heading back into the now thinning crowd. The bands were finished but some

75

sort of industrial music was now banging through the system. Loudly.

'Fuck me, what is that noise?' said Ronnie. 'I can't have a lot more of it – let's find him and get out of here. This is enough to give you the horrors, I don't know about psychotropic drugs. Here we go H, up these stairs mate.'

H didn't much like the look of the scene in the toilets either, but he and Ronnie surged all the way in anyway; there was nowhere else left to look. They established, with relief, that their friend was not a part of any of the huddles about the place, and went knocking door-to-door along the stalls.

'John, you in there?' shouted H. 'It's me, H, and Ronnie...are you in here?'

They heard a low moan and a kind of whimpering coming from the end stall, and banged on it harder. 'John,' said Ronnie, 'is that you? You in there, mate? Open up. It's me, Ronnie, and H – open up.' The moaning continued but the door stayed shut.

'Alright Ron, stand back mate. That sounds like him to me.'

H shouldered the door; it burst open straight away – and there was Shy Nervous John Viney, sitting on the toilet with his arms wrapped around his stomach, rocking back and forth, looking at the floor of the cubicle with ferocious intensity.

'Fuck me,' whispered Ronnie, 'have a look at the state of him. This might be a good time to leave the "Shy Nervous" bit out, no?'

'Yep,' said H. 'John, it's me and Ronnie, mate. What you doing in here? Are your guts hurting? Speak to me son, what's happening?'

Their friend's upturned face, when it came, shocked H and Ronnie both; it was more like a gurning, tortured mask than the face they knew; the eyes and cheeks were red raw –

he'd obviously been doing a fair bit of crying, and pulling at his cheeks.

'Hello boys,' said Shy Nervous John, 'alright?'

His head was down, his gaze redirected back to the ground, before anyone could answer. H and Ronnie looked at one another, each one mirroring the other's anxiety.

'Looks like he's completely lost the fucking plot,' said Ronnie. 'What do we do?'

'Talk to him, Ron, we've just got to talk to him. Quietly.'

They both went further into the cubicle and crouched down closer to the ground. Ronnie took the lead. 'Alright John, we've been looking for you mate. What you been doing in here? Is your stomach OK? What are you looking at on the floor – what is it?'

'Them. I'm looking at them,' said Shy Nervous John, pointing to the floor. Neither Ronnie nor H could see anything. 'What mate…there's nothing there. Just floor tiles – is that what you're looking at?'

'No, them,' said Shy Nervous John, '*them* fucking things.'

'He means the silverfish mate – look, in the grouting between the tiles, there's silverfish,' said H.

'Ah, OK mate, got you – you're looking at the silverfish, yeah?'

'Yeah, that's it, silverfish. I couldn't remember what they were called. Silverfish. There's thousands of them in here, millions of them. Look how horrible they are – all slithery and silver. Swarming all over the gaff. Ron… I've got to ask you something.'

'Anything mate – crack away.'

'Have they got teeth? Them things – have they got teeth?'

'I'm not sure mate. We'll look it up, when we get home. My brother's got an insect encyclopaedia – we can look up whether they've got teeth or not when we get home, alright?'

'Is that what they are then?'

'What?'

'Insects.'

'Not sure – I assume they're insects. They're little, and creepy-crawly, like insects. Anyway, we'll check. I think we should make a move now mate. Let's not worry about the silverfish till we get back to London. Let's get out of this khazi and find something nice to do – something relaxing.'

'But what if they're not insects, Ron. What if they've got teeth. What if they could get much bigger, like dogs. Or us. And they were all over the khazi and the bath. What if…'

Ronnie moved in closer and put his arm tightly around his friend and held him for a few moments.'Sshhh, it's alright John. We're moving on from them things now mate – we're going home for a nice cup of tea, yeah? Fancy that?'

Shy Nervous John said nothing, but Ronnie felt the tension in John's body relax; he loosened his grip on his friend, who fell once again to staring at the floor, this time more calmly. Ronnie indicated to H with a nod of the head that they should leave the cubicle and leave him to it for a bit.

'He's lost it mate. I think we need to get him to a hospital,' he said. 'Maybe they can pump his stomach and get some sort of shrink to have a look at him.'

'Nah,' said H. 'It's way too late for the pump, and it's two o'clock on a Saturday morning in Amsterdam. What d'you suppose it'll be like in the casualty department? It might be wall-to-wall Shy Nervous Johns. What good would that do him? Anyway, a shrink won't be able to do much for him in our timeframe. I say we get him back to the hostel. Nice and quiet, just me and you can talk to him and reassure him.'

'But they could give him something, they've got experts.'

'No, he don't need all that Ron. He just needs his mates. And some peace and quiet. And a bit of kip. He'll be right as rain in a couple of days. Trust me.'

'Alright mate, if you say so. I…'

'OK Ron, good man. Time to get cracking. You go down into the street and get hold of a cab and I'll bring him down.'

# Saturday

Saturday morning turned out to be sunny and warm – perfect conditions in which to play the beautiful game, on a pitch that Tony Pickett knew from previous experience was perfect for stroking the ball about on. He shambled into the dorm room containing H, Ronnie and John. They were all sound asleep.

'Morning campers. This is your ten o'clock alarm call. I would like to remind you all that the game's scheduled for three. Bus is due at half-twelve. We'll be getting to the Vondelpark nice and early for our warm-up.'

Nobody moved, or batted an eyelid. The room stank of alcohol fumes and weed, and the floor was strewn with clothes, beer cans and polystyrene Chinese takeaway boxes. Also on the floor was Shy Nervous John Viney, curled up in a ball among the detritus, twitching in his sleep. Pickett had been in charge, however nominally, of a few of these tours now, and he thought he'd seen it all – but this lot had really pushed the boat out.

He moved to H's bunk, knowing that if he could get him going the rest would follow.

'H, time to get up mate. Wakey wakey.'

Nothing. H was dead to the world. They were all dead to the world.

Pickett pulled up one of H's eyelids and blew into it. H responded by flinging his arm out from his bunk in a sweeping arc, and sitting bolt-upright, banging his head on the bunk above. He emitted a groan that seemed to come from a very deep, dark place.

'Are you with me H? It's time to get everyone up – we've got to start getting ready for the game. I'll bring you some strong coffee, shall I?'

'What time is it?'

'Ten o'clock. What time did you all get in?'

'Not sure, about two or three, I think.'

'Good lads.'

'But we didn't go to sleep until much later, about seven I think. Shy Nervous John had a bit of a bad time, we had to sort him out.'

'What happened?'

'Well, he took something, acid he said it was, and it gave him the horrors.'

'Yes. He doesn't look all that now.'

'Where is he?'

'Down here, on the deck.'

'Fuck, he did say he didn't want to sleep on his bunk. Something about giant fleas coming to get him. He had the proper horrors. Ronnie wanted to take him to the hospital, but we brought him back here instead and talked him down. I can't see us getting him back on his feet in time to play.'

'He can go in goal. The post'll keep him up.'

H laughed. 'You seem very relaxed about all this, Pick.'

'Well, boys will be boys. It's all par for the course H... all par for the course in Amsterdam. The thing with these tours is...you just have to turn up and play for ninety minutes. That's the deal. That's what I get paid for.'

'They're paying you?'

'Yep.'

'Fucking hell, I had no idea. How do you get away with it?'

'It's a doddle mate, I just fulfil all our contractual agreements to the letter.'

'What would you say our chances are, of getting a result?'

'Zero. Not a chance in hell mate – even if you'd all trained properly and not wrecked yourselves with booze and drugs. A lot of the boys we'll be playing have been through the Ajax youth academy. They can drop a tennis ball onto your nan's head from fifty yards.'

81

'Fuck. So a bit of the old Norman Hunter treatment won't do it – you know, getting in amongst them?'

'You won't get anywhere near them mate, forget it. They'll disappear like wisps of smoke while you're still shaping up to bite them in the leg.'

H was silent for a few moments, before launching himself off the bunk and forcing himself upright.

'Thanks Pick, superb pep talk. I'm raring to go now. I'll get my mates ready.'

'Good.'

'What about the rest of them, the younger blokes? How are they getting on?'

'Well, I think some of them haven't been to bed at all – I know for a fact that Billy Marshall's little firm have been on the whizz all night. I'm just hoping they stay on it long enough to get them through the game. They can sleep it off on the bus to Germany tomorrow.'

\*\*\*

The game finally got under way at three-fifty. Anglers Athletic managed to get nine outfield players onto the pitch, with Shy Nervous John propped up in goal making for a respectable ten-man team. This was good enough for Pickett, who'd expected a worse outcome. Billy, leading the line with his usual gusto and Ronnie, as staunchly unpassable as ever in central defence, were the only Anglers players with anything about them. But when Ronnie poleaxed the silky Dutch right-winger from behind twenty minutes in, and was sent off for his troubles, low expectation turned to outright disaster. H – despite his size and his tendency to go in with bone-crunching tackles, still fancied himself as the skilful midfield general – puffed and shouted his way through the rest of the half as best he could. But it was not enough to keep the Dutch out, and the Anglers retired to the dressing room six-nil down.

'Right,' said Pickett as they sucked on their oranges, 'I will say this lads: you are holding your heads up. You are definitely holding your heads up. Six down, against players of that quality, and with the state you're all in, is a reasonable achievement. I think we can still get something out of this game.'

The laughter that greeted this was so infectious with even Ronnie, who'd been sulking like a bear with a sore head since his sending off, joined in.

'And what would that be Pick, you dozy great fucking lump?' said H. 'I mean, what would you classify as "getting something" out of this situation?'

'Keeping them to single-figures H, keeping them to single figures. If we keep them to three goals and they total nine we can walk out of here with our heads held high.'

'And how do you suppose we might do that?' said Ronnie.

'I know,' said Billy. 'We can get one of them bags of sand we passed in the car park and put it in goal instead of Shy Nervous John. He can have a nice little rest second half and we can regroup. I see no reason we shouldn't nick this one 7-6. I've still got a bit of whizz left, if anyone…'

'Alright Bill, thanks for your input,' said Pickett. 'By the way, how are you feeling John?'

'Sort of like Jesus did when they took him down off the cross, only worse. And my old man ain't God.'

'Don't fancy the second half then mate?'

'No, I don't. You'll have to find someone else to go in goal.'

'Any volunteers?' said Pickett.

'Yes, go on then, I'll go in,' said H. 'I might get a better view of things and be able to marshal the defence a bit better from there.'

'Good man, that's the spirit,' said Pickett. 'Sound tactical reasoning as well. Now we're getting somewhere.'

***

The second half began with Anglers fielding a nine-man team with H in goal. With him out of the way the central midfield felt to the Dutch players as wide open as a savannah, and they stroked and flicked and juggled the ball at their leisure, toying with the Englishmen for all they were worth but keeping things on a gentlemanly level by scoring only five more goals, when good taste dictated that they absolutely had to.

Billy scored a wonder consolation goal with five minutes left, surprising the keeper with a thirty-yard screamer. He followed this up with a head butt to the bridge of the keeper's nose when he took too long to give the ball back, and was sent off. The game ended 11-1, with eight Anglers men standing on the field.

Pickett stood on the side-lines and clapped his players off, patting each of them on the back as they headed towards the dressing room.

'Right lads, team talk on the bus tomorrow. But for now, I'll just say this: if we can play on Monday like we did for the last ten minutes here, we'll give the Germans something to think about. That is for certain. Hamburg here we come.'

# Sunday

'John's feeling a bit fragile, do us a favour and drop out the "Shy Nervous" bit when you talk to him from now on, will you boys? He ain't feeling all that clever,' said H to the company assembled on the bus as John staggered, oblivious, out of the hostel and approached the door of the vehicle.

Everybody nodded their assent to H's appeal, though general hilarity broke out when John scrambled aboard and half-walked, half-crawled to the back seat and threw himself down, moaning gently.

'Come on, Shy Nervous John,' said Billy. 'Liven up mate. Come and have a game of cards. We'll be playing kalooki once we've got underway.'

'What the fuck's kalooki?'

'Well, it's a card game, Shy Nervous John. You play with two decks, it's a blinding game. Come on, I'll teach you – a free lesson, courtesy of the Billy Marshall card school.'

'I don't play cards, Bill. I don't play games. I don't gamble, I'm not an idiot.'

'Well you've doing a fucking good impression of one, Shy Nervous John. I thought...'

'Bill!' shouted H. 'For fuck's sake, what did I say to you? Leave him alone, he needs a kip.'

Pickett lumbered in through the door, closed it behind him, and whispered in the driver's ear. 'Alright boys, everyone here? Have you done a head count H?'

'Yeah, we're all here Pick – let's get a move on.'

Pickett nodded to the driver; he sparked up the ignition, pulled out of the street and set a course, through driving rain, for the German border.

\*\*\*

The hum of the bus and the bleakness of the view from the window put half of the company to sleep; the other half whooped, hollered, joked and cursed at the Billy Marshall card school. Billy himself showed no sign of slowing down, amphetamines or no amphetamines. His shouting and skylarking eventually woke H from his slumbers, and he found a befuddled-looking Scaffold sitting beside him, flicking through a porn magazine.

'Alright Scaff?' said H. 'What's the matter, had enough of the cards? Has Bill taken all your money?'

'Nearly,' said Scaffold. 'I've nearly done it all. He's murder. I'm his best mate, and he still absolutely slaughtered me. No mercy.'

'Got enough left for Hamburg?' said H. 'I can help you out if you need it.'

'No, you're alright mate, ta. I'll get by,' said Scaffold.

'How much did he take off you?'

'Only about a score.'

'Only about a score? Fuck me, your old man must be looking after you. You still helping him out on the tipper?'

'Yeah, he lets me drive it when we're on a site. I've still got nearly a year before I can go for my heavy goods license though, but he gives me bits and pieces to do. Anyway, he can afford it – he's earning bundles. He's not in your old man's league of course, but...'

'No, my old man's an absolute nutter, no doubt about that. Twelve hours a day he drives, and then if you put all the ducking and diving on top – you know, forging invoices and all that. He's caked-up, he don't know what to do with all the money.'

'You going in with him then? I heard he wanted to expand, get another lorry. Hawkins and Hawkins, that's the idea ain't it? You'll be as rich as him soon,' said Scaff.

'Well...I dunno, mate. He's all gung-ho about it, but...'

'But what?'

'I don't really fancy it, Scaff. Not for years and years, not like him and your old man.'

'Why not? Have you gone potty?' said The Scaffold. 'How else you going to get hold of that sort of money, start robbing banks?'

'Money ain't everything Scaff. You know, I...'

H was interrupted by a shout of 'Yes! Yes! Fucking yes! Have that, you fucking mongrels!'

'Sounds like Billy's cleaned up,' said The Scaffold.

'Driver...Pick,' shouted Billy, standing on his chair, pointing wildly. 'Look, it says "Oldenburg Services" five kilometres. Let's stop, I'm dying for a slash.'

'No, we need to push on to Hamburg. The weather ain't getting any better. The driver's getting the hump, he needs to get home,' said Pickett.

'Tell him if he stops for half hour I'll treat him,' said Billy. 'I'm absolutely fucking caked-up with money here. Come on Pick, a quick stop. I'll buy everyone a drink. What harm can it do?'

\*\*\*

The interior of the service station was spotless; it was less stinky and much classier-looking than they were used to in England. Half the boys had been drinking beer on the bus and headed straight for the toilets. The rest zeroed-in on the café at the centre of the establishment.

Billy pressed a twenty pound note into H's hand. 'Get the drinks in, will you mate – I've heard they're stricter here than they are in Amsterdam. They want to see your passport and everything.'

'Fuck off Bill. Get them yourself – or get your man Pickett to do the honours. I'm going for a little mooch about, don't get anything for me. I need to clear my head.

I'm going for a walk. No thieving, Bill. Just sit and have a nice drink – no thieving.'

H and Ronnie took a turn around the perimeter of the building – John was dead to the world at the back of the bus – and took in the sounds and sights. Both were startled to hear German being spoken around them, a language they'd only ever heard in war films, spoken by actors playing Nazis, and it unnerved them.

'It's fucking weird here Ron, ain't it?' said H.

'It certainly is mate, the place is crawling with Germans. It's like being stuck in the middle of *Operation Crossbow*. Takes a bit of getting used to, I should think.'

'Maybe it's alright in Hamburg, do you think they all speak English there, like they do in Amsterdam?'

'I ain't got a clue mate,' said Ronnie. 'But I've heard it can be a bit tasty. I think we should keep our wits about us, and keep an eye on Billy Marshall. Fuck knows what sort of trouble him and Scaff will get into if they start giving it, with the old anti-German football songs and all that.'

'They can like it or lump it, as far as I'm concerned. Let's get back inside and see if we can get this lot all back on the bus.'

They returned to the café to the strains of 'Two world wars, one world cup, doo-dah, doo-dah…' and the sight of Pickett replenishing a tableful of glasses with schnapps; he and the quick-learning Dutch driver were leading the singing with gusto. Ronnie stood and shook his head. H just laughed.

'Good to see you keeping the boys in trim for Tuesday's game, Pick,' said H.

'Well, I do my best H, you know me.'

'Yep, that I do. What do you reckon, Pick, one for the road, then pile back on the bus?'

'Sounds like a plan H.'

'Good man. Pour one for me. And don't forget the bottle.'

\*\*\*

They pulled up outside the place they were staying at three o'clock. Pickett, a little the worse for wear, addressed his men from the front of the bus before letting them go.

'Right gentlemen. In we go. A nice shower and an early night are the order of the day here, I think. We need to regroup and get ourselves in order for Tuesday's game. We don't want a repeat of that shambles in Amsterdam, do we? We need to give a good account of ourselves against the Germans.'

'Is that why you've filled us all up with schnapps, Pick?' said Ronnie.

Pickett ignored him. 'So what I'm saying to you, boys, is let's keep it nice and tidy tonight. Training tomorrow, twelve o'clock. You can go out on the town and let your hair down on Tuesday, after the game. Do this for me please boys. If we don't turn up for the game, or let the opposition get into double figures again, I'll be fucked. They won't let me come again. Do this for me, yeah? It's not like I ain't been good to you all. What do you think?'

'Blinding,' said Billy,' Superb. You can count on us, coach.'

'Grand. Lead them in and get them through reception, will you H?'

H opened the door and asked them to collect their bags and wait in front of the hostel. As they filed out he moved to the back of the bus and roused John.

'We're here John, liven up mate. Sort yourself out. We're going into the hostel now. Early night tonight. Pick's orders. Fun and games postponed till Tuesday. Alright?'

89

'Yeah,' said John, shaking himself awake. 'Sweet as a nut. Nice quiet night in. Got it.'

He thanked H for his trouble, shambled out into the car park and approached Billy as he waited to file into the building.

'Here, Bill,' he said, 'you still holding any of that whizz?'

# Sunday Evening

'I'll go on my own then if I have to, you fucking melts. I haven't come all this way to have an "early night" ten minutes from the Reeperbahn, just so this fat ponce Pickett can keep the club sweet.'

H and Ronnie looked at one another, and around the cramped, tiny hostel room. It was seven o'clock, and both had to admit John had a point.

'Come on chaps, liven yourselves up. Alright, I went a bit strong in Amsterdam the other night, but I've learned my lesson. I won't be eating any fistfuls of acid tonight – scout's honour. But it's wall-to-wall dirty women out there, and all the strong German beer you can drink, and God knows what else. What you two going to do, sit here all-night knitting cardigans for your mums?'

H took a deep breath and sighed. 'Alright John, fair enough. I'm having it. Ron?'

'Did he just say something about "wall-to-wall dirty women"?' said Ronnie.

'I believe he did,' said H.

'Right. I'll go for a quick mooch about and get another bottle of schnapps for Pickett. That ought to settle his nerves,' said Ronnie. 'By the time he's worked his way through that we'll be firing on all cylinders on the Reeperbahn, and he won't give a fuck, or remember anything about it in the morning.'

'Blinding,' said John. 'Absolutely blinding. I'm going to brush my teeth – don't be long, Ron.'

\*\*\*

They finally crept out the back way at nine o'clock; leaving Pickett and his new Dutch driver friend in the cafeteria, hammering the schnapps.

'This way boys,' said Ronnie, consulting his map. 'Shouldn't take us long.' The air was crackling with tension, Sunday night though it was: weird cooking smells and unfamiliar sounding sirens filled the air, and very dodgy looking characters filled the street. The boys were buzzing, and ready for anything, when five minutes into their walk they heard, coming from behind them, 'H! Slow down mate, we're coming!'

It was Billy Marshall and The Scaffold, running to catch up with them – Billy, high and exhilarated, moving like quicksilver and leading the way with The Scaffold, plodding on lugubriously in a sort of slow-motion jog, in his wake.

H, Ronnie and John stopped walking, and turned to face them.

'Fucking hell Bill,' shouted H as the two boys closed in on them. 'What you doing here? Who told you you could come?'

'I did,' said John. 'He helped me out with a bit of whizz, so I told him he could come. What harm can it do?'

'What harm can it do? We're going into the middle of the Reeperbahn with this loose cannon and you're asking what harm it can do? He don't know how to behave mate, he's a nutter, that's what. The Scaff's alright, he's solid, he knows how to look after himself. But Billy Marshall? For fuck's sake, John.'

Billy caught up, looking like a bright-eyed, joyful puppy about to be taken for a walk.

'Alright boys?' he said. 'Where to first? I'm absolutely fucking gagging for it. Shall we see if we can dig out a bit of whizz from somewhere to get us started?'

'No, Bill,' said H, knowing it would be very difficult to shake the kid off now. 'What we're going to do is find somewhere for a nice drink and see what's what. The night is young. We don't want you going off half-cocked on drugs, like John did the other night, and fucking things up for the rest of us. You got me?'

'Aye aye captain,' said Billy with a salute. 'Your wish is my command.'

'Right then, the Reeperbahn starts just round the corner. Let's plot up somewhere with a few beers,' said Ronnie. 'Follow me.'

They walked, past prostitutes, slimy looking pimps, gawping tourists and wrecked-looking drug hounds. As they turned towards their destination they noted bodies on the ground and a fight petering out, between what looked like some British sailors and a group of biker-ish looking locals.

'Go on boys, let them fucking have it,' shouted Billy. He wrapped his arm around The Scaff's shoulders and the pair of them went straight into 'Rule Britannia, Britannia rules the waves, Britons never never never shall be…'

'Alright boys, that'll do. We don't want to get sucked into all that nonsense,' said H. 'Let's go in here.' He led the way into a nondescript, unadorned bar full of people sucking on huge steins of beer.

'We'll have five of them please, guvnor,' said H to the barman, who understood the gist if not the language of H's request. The beers arrived and John, Billy and The Scaff took theirs with both hands and performed a staggering-under-heavy-weights mime show as they made their way to a table, next to another occupied by three heavily made-up teenage girls.

Ronnie engaged them immediately. 'Any of you ladies speak English?' he asked, leaning in towards them.

They looked at him as if he'd just fallen out of the sky. 'Sprechen sie Deutsch?' one of them said.

'No, afraid not darling. We're from London, we only speak English. You know, English, like Kevin Keegan. F.C.

Hamburg. European Footballer of the Year for the last two years. Kevin Keegan?'

'Ah, Kevin Keegan,' they chorused '*Mighty Mouse.*'

'Is that what you call him?' said Ronnie, 'Funny.'

'Yes, well we Germans do have a sense of humour – whatever you English say,' said the girl who'd spoken before.

'Blinding. Lovely. Can I ask you a question?' said Ronnie.

He took their silence as a yes.

'Are you girls prostitutes?'

'We might be,' said the talkative one.

Billy piped up: 'What's the best place to get hold of drugs round here then girls. Whizz…you know, speed. Any ideas?'

'Just down the street – go left out of here, until you get to Titty Twister. Fifty metres. Next door to that there is a bar. The bikers there will help you.'

'Now we're talking,' said John. 'Come on then Bill, let's go and have some of that. We'll be back in a minute, boys.' The two of them stood up and headed for the door. Before they got through it H rose as well, and said, 'Hold up boys, I'm coming with you. Just to keep an eye on things. Scaff, you stay here with Ronnie. We won't be long.'

***

They found the bar with no name exactly where the girls said it would be, right next to Titty Twister. It made the place they'd just left look like the Café De Paris in Leicester Square. It was grimmer than anything they'd seen in Amsterdam, or London, or even Manchester: it was barely lit at all, filled with the noise of some sort of ear-splitting Germanic rock, and plotted up at the bar was a string of half a dozen or so of the dirtiest, worst dressed individuals imaginable, drinking beer and laying on the menace with a trowel.

H and the boys stood for a few moments at the threshold. Their appearance didn't exactly make the place go quiet, like in a Western when the good guy barrels into a bar of bad guys, but all faces turned to them and stared hard, daring them to venture any further in.

'Fuck me, have a look at this lot,' shouted John above the noise. 'It's been a fucking long while since this little lot have seen a bar of soap.'

'They ain't nothing John, don't worry about them,' said Billy. 'They're fuck-all without their soppy leather jackets. Let's just get hold of some gear and get back to the others. Them girls Ronnie's lining up look like they're raring to go.'

'Alright boys, just slow down a bit,' said H. 'Don't get agitated, don't let them think you're scared. It's just a bit of business,' said H. He scanned the room and quickly picked out the most composed and formidable man in the company, sitting at a table at the back of the room. 'There's your man boys, he'll be the guvnor. You two go and have a word with him – I'll hang back and keep an eye on things from here.'

'What, you mean like when you "marshalled" the defence the other day from the goal line? I don't recall that went very well,' said Billy.

'Behave yourself, silly bollocks,' said H. 'Let's just deal with the matter in hand. John, go over there and buy your gear will you, we don't want to be stuck in this shithouse all night with boy wonder here.'

\*\*\*

The Scaffold was feeling way out of his depth in the scenario unfolding around him in the other bar. He ploughed on with his beer, ordered another and watched and learned from Ronnie, who seemed to be negotiating terms with the girls with one of them sitting on his lap and another nibbling at his ear. He understood Ronnie to be thrashing out a group rate for all of them. He had no idea what that might turn out to be, but hoped that he had enough money left to put in his whack.

Then he recalled with satisfaction H's promise to help him out if necessary, and was smiling to himself in anticipation when he heard what he thought was Billy's voice, calling from the street. He went to the door for a look, and saw just enough to grasp that things had gone wrong before a beer bottle came spinning through the air and smashed into his face, knocking him backwards and down onto the ground. Billy burst into the bar a second later, wild-eyed and panting, and shouted 'Ron, out here! Quick! It's all gone off – H is bang in trouble.'

Ronnie arrived in the street five seconds later, and saw H going toe-to-toe thirty yards away from where he was with three greasy-looking bikers, gruesome as hell and twice as ugly. They had him surrounded in a triangle, and were limiting him to defensive arm movements against the blows from the bike chains they were wielding. They looked frightening and formidable, cursing in guttural German and doing their best to force him down onto the ground, where they could finish him off.

But H was standing. His arms, torso and head were taking a fearsome hammering, and there was blood gushing from cuts to his scalp and forehead, but he was observing the golden rule: never go down.

Ronnie was ten yards out, rushing headlong to H's aid, before he even knew what he was doing. Running on sheer instinct and intuition, he picked up a lightweight metal chair from outside a café without slowing down and thrust it with main force into the face of one of the bikers; one of its legs went straight into the man's left eye – he went down onto his knees immediately, clutching at the area around his eye with both hands. Ronnie brought the chair down firmly onto his back, threw it into the road and brought his heel down onto the man's neck.

H was now up against a café window, working hard to wrest the chain from the hands of one of his assailants while the other went at him with sickening body punches. Ronnie went in low against this one, throwing his centre of gravity off by pulling at his legs and tipping him over onto his back, then straddling his torso and treating him to a series of head butts to the nose and cheekbones. The biker begged for mercy, as far as Ronnie could tell, but was shown none. He stopped moving; the lights were out.

He moved closer to H, whose struggle over the chain with a stinking, hairy lump as big as the side of a house had reached fifty-fifty, and nutted the man-mountain on the side of the head, squashing and splitting the softer tissue around the ear. His grip on the chain loosened momentarily; H ripped it from his grasp and belayed him with it with savage blows until he went down in a heap.

H and Ronnie were now side by side in the street, bent over double, breathing hard, recovering from their exertions. A crowd had gathered on the other side of the street to watch the fun and games, and watched with rapt interest as Billy, pulling The Scaffold along behind him by the arm, surged past H and Ronnie and back to the door of the biker's bar.

'Come on then,' shouted Billy into the dark interior, in which a few of the leather-clad denizens were considering their options. 'Have you fucking mongrels had enough yet or you want some more? Get out here.'

A barrage of sirens set up in the near distance, bringing H to his senses.

'Where's John?' he shouted. John emerged from a shop window on the other side of the street, limping heavily, his face bloodied. He was cut and heavily swollen about the mouth.

'I'm here, H. All present and correct. We should make a move – sounds like Old Bill are on their way.'

He joined H and Ronnie, and the three of them moved back along to where Billy and The Scaffold were standing. H's attention was caught by a tram coming down the street, slowing down and coming to a halt at a stop.

'Bill, Scaff. Get on the tram,' shouted H. 'Sharpish. Say your goodbyes and get on this fucking tram. Now!'

The Scaffold pulled Billy back from the doorway of the bar, backed him up towards the doors of the tram, and pulled him up inside. Billy was shaking all over with rage, and gesticulating wildly. The tram doors closed; he administered his parting shot as they pulled away: 'Don't fuck with South London,' he said.

They all collapsed onto the seats of the half-empty carriage, beginning to calm down, with the exception of Billy, who H was learning seemed to be hyped-up and mental at all times – amphetamines or no amphetamines.

'Well, that was lively,' said Billy, 'We done well there boys – our backs was against the wall, and...'

'Well, mine was, thanks to you, you soppy little bastard,' said H.

'What?' said Billy. 'Was I supposed to let him take the piss out of us like that?'

'Not necessarily mate, no, not necessarily. But did you have to nut the geezer and start singing *Rule Britannia* in his face?'

'He did what?' said Ronnie.

'Well, it was all starting to go a bit wobbly,' said H. 'The geezer obviously didn't want to serve them...'

'So Billy took matters into his own hands,' said John. 'And the rest is history.'

# Monday

Pickett finally crawled out of bed at two o'clock in the afternoon, two hours after training was supposed to start. He made a tour of the hostel, to see what he could see. He had little recall of the previous evening's events, beyond his having made a concerted effort to improve Anglo-Dutch relations, and was now perplexed to find no one at home.

'Seen anything of my party?' he asked the hostel receptionist,' I can't find them anywhere.'

'They came down an hour ago, most of them,' said the receptionist. 'I think they went to the café over the road for something to eat. I didn't like to ask last night,' she said, 'but they looked like they were just returning from the Battle of Normandy. I asked if I should phone ambulances, but...'

'Okey Dokey,' said Pickett. 'Got it. Boys will be boys. I'll deal with it. Did they cause you any problems?'

'No, on the contrary. They were in high spirits, and all very charming. No trouble at all.'

'Alright, thanks my love. I'll go and have a look at them. I have a feeling we'll be leaving early, probably later today, so if you'd be kind enough to prepare the bill.'

***

The bus crossed the border into the Netherlands at eight o'clock, without a passport check.

'Just as well,' said John as they crossed over.

'What you talking about John?' said Ronnie.

'I'm just saying, it's just as well they didn't do a passport check back there.'

'Why?'

'Because I've lost mine. Can't find the fucking thing anywhere.'

'Well, you'll need it to get out of Holland, and you'll definitely need it at our border. You know what they're like.'

'Yeah, well, I'll cross that bridge when I come to it. I'll have a word with Pickett.'

It was still raining. The evening was dark, and windy, with no sign of the sky.

'Fuck it,' said Billy, very loudly, to no one in particular. 'It's bound to be another poxy crossing on that ferry. What a nightmare.'

The whole bus groaned, and thanked him for the reminder, and huddled down to try and get a little sleep while they could.

***

'We can't just leave him here on his own,' said H as the bus departed Amsterdam after dropping John and Pickett off.

'Yeah, we can,' said Ronnie. 'Pickett will get him to the consulate and they'll sort him out. They'll give him thirty quid subsistence money to see him alright – he'll think Christmas has come early. Then they'll put him on the boat home with a cut-up passport. He'll have to pay them back and apply for a new one when he gets back. That's what they do with nutters like him who lose the plot when they're over here. All day long, mate, all day fucking long.'

'How come you know all this?' said H.

'I know everything,' said Ronnie.

'Alright then, clever bollocks, riddle me this: what are you doing working for thirteen quid a week in a poxy warehouse?'

'Biding my time.'

'Until when? Until what?'

'Until I can figure out how to manage proper money.'

'What, by heaving hundredweight sacks onto the back of a lorry?'

'Well, it keeps me fit mate, as you've seen. But what I'm really doing is finding out how the business works. The accountant there's a bit of a ginger, I think. Anyway, I've been treating him to a pint or two at lunchtime and he's been showing me how the books work – you know, ledgers, double entry book keeping and all that.'

'You sure a couple of pints is all you've been treating him to?' said H.

'Behave yourself H.'

'Alright son, fair do's. But what's the plan, what are you going to do with yourself?'

'Once I know what I'm doing I'm going to get a market stall. I know a geezer who wants to sell his pitch down East Lane.'

'Selling what?'

'Toiletries, house cleaning stuff for housewives. They buy all that shit every week, so you get never-ending repeat business. It's a guaranteed earner mate. I'll be getting hold of so much money after a couple of months I won't know what to do with it. Every sort in south London will be throwing herself at me.'

\*\*\*

They boarded the huge *Pride of Rotterdam*, for their second all-night North Sea battering in less than a week, at eleven o'clock. Billy and the rest of the team headed straight for the bar to repeat all their mistakes of the previous week. H bought two coffees and steered Ronnie to a quiet corner; there were things he needed to say.

'I dunno Ron, I've been thinking about what you said on the bus. There's got to be more to life.'

'More than what, being your own guvnor, getting hold of massive amounts of money and chasing the girls round – or getting them to come to you? Have you gone mental?'

101

'No, I fucking have not. I'm talking about doing something big, something serious. Something important.'

'Like what?'

'Putting yourself on the line. Taking risks. Excitement…but for a reason. Fighting for something really worth fighting for. I don't mean all this silly bollocks we've been doing over here this week, but…'

'You're talking about growing up mate, no? Making your life have some meaning.'

'Yep. That. I can't just be fucking about the way I have been. I'll be twenty soon. I need to get my teeth into something, and it ain't being a tipper driver.'

'So…'

'The Army. I'm going to join up. For real this time. I know I fucked it up before, but I was only a kid then. I'm joining up, when we get back. I want to get my feet under the table for a bit and then apply for the Paras.'

'Makes sense, H. I reckon…'

'No mate, I'm not asking you to tell me what you think. Listen to what I'm saying, I'm being serious. I think you should come in with me. You can always run your little market stall down the lane when you get out. We can go in together, do ourselves proud. Come in with me.'

# That's Life

# November 1995

H returned to the table beaming like the cat that got the cream, put down his tray of drinks and handed them out. Two glasses of wine and two gin and tonics for the girls, five beers for the boys and tonic water, with ice and a slice, for his beloved Julie. He raised his glass and made a toast to the bride and groom, who were being tracked around the reception venue by a pesky photographer who would not leave them alone. H was feeling the vibe, getting the party moving.

'To the beautiful bride and the not so beautiful groom,' he shouted, winking across the room at Billy Marshall as he downed his pint and turned his attention back to his drinking companions: 'Who's for another?'

'Slow down H,' said Julie, 'Rome wasn't built in a day, and there's plenty of wine on the tables.'

But H was irrepressible; he was not for slowing, and he was not about to start drinking wine. Even the thought of the best man's speech he still had to deliver – things had not always gone H's way on that front – couldn't blunt his enthusiasm. Ignoring his wife's advice, he surged back to the bar and returned with another round.

'Babe, relax,' he said as he bent down and gave Julie a loving kiss on the cheek, 'everything's under control.' He placed his hand on her swollen belly, the primary cause of the high-energy bouncing around he was doing these days. Julie smiled. Her husband seemed more and more like the old H, the H she had fallen in love with as a young girl. He was happy, funny, and full of life. But he wasn't the kind of man who would show solidarity with his pregnant woman by jumping on the wagon for nine months, and didn't expect it, but she knew he'd be there when it mattered, when the boy – H was already calling him 'Little Ronnie', and would brook no argument on the matter – was growing up.

More guests started to roll in and were greeted warmly by the bride and groom, while H chatted with the group at his table. Billy Marshall had arranged to seat representatives of the old Angler's Athletic crew together. It had been a while since they'd done anything like this and H was loving every moment. They made an odd crowd these days: H's best mate, the ultra-successful property tycoon Ronnie Ruddock and Tara, his high-society wife, sat next to the archetypal south London wastrel, Confident John Viney, today accompanied by old friend and long-time drug buddy Jessica, who he dragged out with him whenever there was an awkward social situation to deal with. Then there was Chris 'The Scaffold' Casey, Tony Pickett and both their wives, Debbie and Sandra.

'Oi, H, you practiced your speech?' said The Scaffold.

'Don't fuck it up H, you know how Her Ladyship over there likes everything to be just right,' added Pickett in a passing reference to the highly-strung bride who, it was well known, had expressed reservations about Billy's choice of best man.

'Don't you lot start, I've got it all covered. Me and Julie went through it last night,' said H, pausing to finish his second beer, 'and there'll be no slagging off the bride on my watch, thank you very much.' This was Billy's second marriage but Jennifer's first and H, having been afforded the honour of being best man, wanted to do his best to make sure it was a day she would always remember – for the right reasons.

'What you going to say then H?' said Ronnie. 'I hope you're not going to try and use any of them long words you did at our wedding?'

'He don't know any big words,' said Sandra Pickett.

'Julie might have lined a couple up for him,' said Ronnie. 'She knows loads of big words now she's studying sociology, don't you Ju?'

'Alright, alright. Very funny. Who's for another?' said H.

'H, slow down, you can't keep going at this pace,' said Julie.

'Maybe not babes, maybe not, but I can try,' said H with the same impish smile that hadn't left him all day.

The last of the guests were now in place and the sit-down meal began. Wine and champagne were poured by the waiters, but H again made his way to the bar, this time for a scotch. The maid of honour, bridesmaids and their friends from the bride's side of the family were in a huddle, crowding the bar, laughing and giggling like underage school girls in a pub.

'This looks like trouble,' said H, after ordering up his drink.

The huddle opened and welcomed H into their circle. Introductions were made, glasses were chinked, and the old H charm poured forth.

'Well, anyway, here I am girls. What are your other two wishes?' He hadn't updated his flirting lines since the seventies, but they still came in useful when it was time for a bit of fun.

'When's your wife due?' said the Maid of Honour, looking over to the table where Mrs Hawkins was doing a reasonable impersonation of a beached whale.

'Next week, so anytime really. I'm hoping she won't get all previous and go into labour during my speech.' H was just getting into his stride now, but the Master of Ceremonies was beckoning him with a look that said 'Showtime.'

'Shit,' said H, 'I think I'm on. See you later girls; wish me luck.'

'Good luck,' they said in unison.

H took his place at the top table and the formalities began; he was up straight away, and had barely pulled the paper with the scribbled speech from his inside pocket when the heckling began. Wouldn't have wanted it any other way. His mates were in fine fettle, and enjoying the experience of seeing their man on show, so the heckling continued as each wit tried to outshine the last. H wanted them to have fun and didn't want to slow them down too much, so he waited until the initial energy subsided before starting.

'Hello everyone…so, when I was writing this speech…'

'Jesus, he writes as well,' said The Scaffold. 'Nah,' another voice shouted, 'Julie grips his hand and moves the pencil for him. I hope you got it all down in the big block-capitals, Ju.' Laughter all round.

Julie had insisted that there be absolutely no swearing or filthy stories – women and children being present – and H was old-school enough to know that swearing would be poor form, but he could now no longer quash his natural responses.

'Yeah, well, they wasted a good arsehole when they put teeth in your mouth son.'

Julie looked mortified. H knew he'd gone a little too far, but he used the space opened by the ensuing laughter to crack on.

'Well, as I was saying, when I was writing this speech Billy asked me not to mention any of his mess-ups or embarrassing moments, and make absolutely no reference to any of his ex-girlfriends, or passing fancies, or gambling habits, or lost weekends. So that's me done then,' he said, pretending to put the speech back into his pocket.

More laughter and another wave of heckling followed before H could continue.

It wasn't the best best-man's speech he'd ever delivered, but it was far from the worst. The drunken, incoherent, over-wordy one he gave at Ronnie and Tara's wedding was hard to beat on that score; the general consensus was that it would never be beaten.

Julie showed H a book on what to include, which ensured all the usual references were there. Thanks to the organisers, messages from absent friends, old stories about the groom, marital advice to the newlyweds, a tribute to the maid of honour and bridesmaids - who all gave H a raucous cheer and a wave.

'And last, but by no means least, my congratulations to the bride, who I shall be placing under arrest later because looking that gorgeous cannot be legal.'

When the applause died down H lifted his pint for the final toast.

'Ladies and gentlemen, please raise your glasses to the bride and groom.'

The guests followed H's lead.

'To the bride and groom.'

***

H kept the drinks flowing for everyone as the night wore on, and even the diabolical DJ – in H's opinion, at least – couldn't dampen his spirits. But he was trying his best. The speakers blasted out a relentless stream of Oasis, Blur and the rest of the current fashionable Brit pop bands. And if it wasn't the Britpoppers it was some variant of the metronomic bang bang bang noise they called techno. The point came when he could take no more, and he made a beeline for the DJ.

'Listen son. I've had enough of all this bollocks – there are people here over fifteen years of age, how about something for us?'

'What kind of thing you after?'

'How about a bit of Tony Newley? Something for the old Londoners.'

'Who?'

'God give me strength. How about Sinatra, I take it you've heard of him?' The DJ raised his eyes to the sky, but did as requested. 'Here's one for the old-timers amongst us,' he announced as he fired up Sinatra's *That's Life*, one of H's favourite tunes. H held out his hand to Julie and swept her onto the dancefloor as the young singletons made for the bar. H was well-known for his Sinatra turns at the microphone at parties, but this was not the time or place. It was time to sing softly into Julie's ear and glide her, as best he could, across the dancefloor.

He was in his element now and, as he twirled his wife around and around, as far as her condition permitted, a crowd formed around them to enjoy the show. Round and round he went, enjoying the smiling faces of the people close to him and new acquaintances alike, until suddenly he saw with a jolt a face that didn't fit; it was the face of a man he knew, and didn't like, who hadn't been invited and had no real business attending the wedding.

*Smethurst. What the fuck is Smethurst doing here?*

H caught the man's eye and his signal of throwing his thumb behind his shoulder, indicating to H that they needed to talk, away from prying eyes and ears.

*What does he want? Only something proper serious could have brought him here.*

The song ended. H gave Julie a peck on the cheek and escorted her back to her seat.

'Put your feet up, babes,' he said. 'I'll be back in a minute. I've just got to see a man about a dog.'

H signalled the man to follow him outside, and they left the room and walked in silence round to the back of the building.

'Right, start talking. This better be fucking good.'

Smethurst – which H always called him due to his resemblance to an old-school TV actor, having no idea of his

111

actual name – was a scruffy, malodorous Brummie with a fondness for the drink who'd been one of H's top informants for years. They were usually very careful to arrange meetings at the most obscure locations possible, at Smethurst's insistence.

'Come on son, let's have it,' said H. 'What's so urgent it's got you out of your hole in the ground?'

'It's about your old mate, Pat O'Leary. He's been tumbled, by the IRA.'

'How do you know?'

'He called me. He didn't know what else to do.'

'Since when have you two been best buddies?'

'We're not, but he dug me out and asked for my number a little while ago, when he got back to London, because he knows I talk to you.'

'He's back? Why didn't he try and contact me? I'm not hard to find.'

'He's holed up somewhere, terrified to go out, or contact you or anyone he knows from the old days, for everyone's safety. Paranoid as fuck, if you ask me Mr Hawkins.'

'OK…so what happened?'

'Three masked gunmen showed up at his house.'

'Then how come he's still alive?'

'He's paranoid these days, like I said – very, very careful. Said he had that new CCTV thing everyone's talking about put into his place, up in Cricklewood, so he saw them coming. I don't know how he got out. Be just like him to have some sort of escape route planned though.'

'How do you know it was the IRA?'

'I don't. It's what he said.'

'How'd he get tumbled?'

'No idea.'

'Where is he?'

'Don't know. He just begged me to come find you. Matter of life and death, no one else to turn to, and all that. I'd say he's moving around a fair bit.'

'No contact details at all?'

'He gave me a post office box number,' said Smethurst, handing over a scrap of paper. 'He checks it every day.'

'OK, son. Thanks. Now get lost.'

H walked back round to the front of the building with the intention of re-joining the party, but found Confident John Viney sitting on the front steps looking – H had long experience of reading the signs – fed up and out of sorts.

'What's happening John?' he said. 'Everything alright?'

'Well, I don't know mate. I'll probably get off in a minute – these things always give me the hump.'

'What things, weddings?'

'Yeah. I always feel a bit out of it.'

'That's because you're a fucking weirdo mate, what I believe they call these days an "outlier".'

'True, mate. Too true.'

'Slowing down with the drugs might help, son. Have you considered that?'

'Too late for all that now mate. Anyway, Julie looks well. And you two look really happy.'

'We are.'

'Lovely. When's the baby due again?'

'Next week, on paper. Seems like it could happen any time though.'

'Got it. I'm really happy for you mate. All them years of disappointment, you've done well to hang in there.'

'Well, you know, I love her. And you know me son, never say die.'

'Yep, they should engrave that on your tombstone, mate: *He Never Said Die. Until He Died. And Here He Lies.*'

'Alright mate, slow down, for fuck's sake. I'm not ready for my box just yet. I'm going to be a dad any day.'

'Yep. Are you going to be in there, to hold her hand, watch him come out, all that game?'

'No, I am not,' said H, 'that's between the mother, the midwife and the new-born. I'll wait outside and go in when everything's quietened down. Why would she want me there anyway? I'd just get in the way. Make her self-conscious. I would've thought that would make it harder for her, not easier.'

'But it's all the rage now. Support your partner. Share in the experience.'

'Partner? Partner my arse. Julie's my wife, we're not in business together.'

'Well, whatever. It's the done thing, though, these days.'

'Well I ain't doing it. As far as I'm concerned, it's a tough enough business as it is. Last thing she needs is me gawping at her and hanging around like a spare wheel. But I'll be there when I'm needed, she knows that. I'll be there, in the waiting room, like my old man was for me.'

\*\*\*

Pat O'Leary first turned up in 1985, not long after H left the army, at one of his and Julie's house parties. He was in the company of Julie's sister Angela; their relationship looked to be on the sketchy side, but he was good-humoured and funny and gave H a run for his money in the life-and-soul-of-the-party stakes. In the weeks and months following he became an established part of H's social circle, and after a mammoth all-night session in the wake of Barry McGuigan's triumph over Eusebio Pedroza at Loftus Road in June, which made him the WBA featherweight champion, the friendship between the two men was sealed. O'Leary, who was keener on boxing even than H and his mates, was a grand man for securing tickets for fights and became a core part of the group that became well-known in London boxing circles over the next few years, their exploits culminating in a legendary trip to Las Vegas – substantially funded by Ronnie Ruddock – for the Bruno v. Tyson fight in 1989.

The relationship between H and O'Leary took a new turn when the latter – who always said he'd left Belfast when he could no longer stomach the daily grind of brutality around him – indicated that he might be persuaded to come forward with information on a young man with IRA connections who'd battered his girlfriend to death in their Battersea flat with a claw hammer. The murderer in question had contacts and a reputation, so everyone in the know was too scared to talk – everyone except O'Leary. He was willing, he told H, to put him in the picture on the understanding that he'd never be called upon as a witness; he knew full well what the Belfast enforcers did to grasses, and often those just accused of being a grass; over the years he'd had plenty of family members and friends who'd felt the full weight of such 'justice'.

H introduced O'Leary to Jake Ardley of the Special Branch, which was then responsible for counter-terrorist investigations. O'Leary had refused Ardley's request to return to Belfast and work undercover, but had agreed to keep his ear to the ground on both sides of the water, and from time to time provided Ardley with handy snippets of intelligence. But that time had been the 1980's, and O'Leary had not been involved with Ardley, or anyone else of his ilk, since then.

O'Leary suddenly dropped off the radar, as far as H and his friends were concerned, in May 1990. It was generally believed that he had to return to Belfast for family reasons, but he neither gave an account of himself nor stayed in touch. So abrupt was his departure from the scene that there was speculation at the Branch that he'd been found out and eliminated by the Provos. But H received a postcard from his friend from New York later in the year, so they knew he was alive at least.

It was now five years, H realised as he drove along John Ruskin Street towards Kennington, since he'd last laid eyes on O'Leary. They met in the basement of one of a row of squatted condemned houses in St Agnes' Place, backing onto Kennington Park, home to a sprawling motley of anarchists, rastafarians and others who could be relied on to provide sympathetic cover for a man looking to keep himself under the radar. H knew the area well – he visited it frequently as a boy on trips to see some cousins who lived in Walworth. Seeing it always triggered memories of the long summer holidays, playing football and chasing girls around the Kennington Park outdoor swimming pool.

O'Leary, H saw with relief, didn't look too bad. He was clearly under a strain, but he didn't look too bad, and the old glint in his eye could still be seen from time to time during their discussion. They said their hellos and O'Leary began with the pleasantries, wanting to catch up. H slowed him down after a minute and a half.

'OK Pat, let's just get to it, shall we? What the fuck is going on?'

'I don't know, to be honest. I haven't been involved with the Branch for donkey's years now. You know that. Why they'd come for me now I don't rightly know.'

'And you're sure it's the Provos, not some other firm you've upset along the way?'

'Not one hundred per cent, but who else would turn up out of the blue with a team like that? Unless...'

'Unless what mate. come on, spit it out.'

'Well there's a lot going on over there at the minute, H. The picture looks unstable. There's the usual feuding and in-fighting, but the peace process is throwing up a lot of discontents. Maybe the Special Branch, or the good old

Royal Ulster Constabulary sprung a leak, you know, to destabilise the process.'

'I thought the RUC had been disbanded,' said H.

'It was, but really they just gave it another name, like they did when they turned the Special Branch into the Anti-Terrorism Branch. A lot of them hate what's happening, maybe they think it's in their interest keep the focus on lawlessness and violence.'

H chewed this over quietly for a while. His boys or the RUC selling out old grasses to destabilise the peace process. It seemed possible, if not probable. Either way it did not sound good at all for the prospects of his old friend.

'Help me H, what the fucking hell am I going to do?' said O'Leary at length. 'Now they're on me they won't stop until I'm dead – they never do.'

'Witness protection?' said H, somewhat feebly.

'Do me a favour, H. I thought we were having a grown-up conversation. I've never had any intention of testifying against them, so I'll never get it. And you know as well as me I wouldn't last ten minutes, not if they've got a source on the inside.'

'Who else knows about your little chats with Ardley, back in the old days?'

'Only my wife. I had to talk to her about it in the end. That's it. Only her, Ardley, and you. It was your idea, remember?'

'You putting me in the frame, son?'

'No. Of course I'm not. You're the only person I trust. That's why I asked Smethurst to alert you.'

'Your wife then?'

'No. No way. We might be separated but she wouldn't, ever. Honestly, she'd die before she grassed me to them. She hates them more than I do.'

'Assuming you're right, why would Ardley or someone else in the Anti-Terrorism Branch be hanging you out to dry?'

'I don't know, mate, but it's the only explanation that makes any sense really. Help me, H. I helped you out, did what you asked. You owe me.'

'You don't need to tell me that, son. I'm on it,' said H, standing up and getting ready to leave. 'Get the fuck out of this place and make yourself scarce.'

'What if I need to contact you?'

'Work just issued me with one of these,' said H, pulling a small mobile phone out of his pocket. 'Look, they're much smaller now, you can carry them around with you. Here's the number, memorise it.'

***

The Pat O'Leary issue was now top of his priorities, and he'd managed to arrange a next day meeting with Jake Ardley, in his Vauxhall office overlooking the river Thames. He pulled his new toy out as he passed The Oval, and punched Ronnie Ruddock's number into it.

'Listen, Ron, couple of things,' he said, still surprised that he could talk to his old friend with minimum fuss, from a tiny phone, driving along, 'something's come up, I'm phoning to put you in the picture, and ask for a favour.'

'I'm all ears, mate.'

'OK – Pat O'Leary has surfaced.'

'Fuck me,' said Ronnie. 'Old Pat. Now there's a blast from the past. How is he – has he got over his hangover from the Bruno fight in Vegas yet?'

'He's in trouble, mate – he's absolutely bang in trouble. To cut a long story short, he's got the IRA, or someone like them, on his case.'

'I didn't know he was involved in all that?'

'Well, he was. Did a bit of work for us, years ago. Not long before he disappeared.'

'OK. Well that don't sound too clever mate. You mean he was a grass? What's your position in all this?'

'My position is I need to try and help him.'

'But ...'

'No but's, Ron – it won't be long before they root him out. Time is of the essence. I can lay all the details out for you later. If they catch him they'll kill him – that is a dot on the card. And I don't think there's much I can to do to stop them.'

\*\*\*

'For fuck's sake Jake, how on earth did they find him? Be straight with me.'

Jake Ardley was a Branch man of almost thirty years standing. It was an area H had never wanted to apply for, given he'd already had a long spell in the army before joining the Met, and hunting down terrorists was no longer on his to-do list. But it was him who'd put O'Leary and Ardley together, and that gave him partial responsibility for the current situation. H never ducked a situation.

'I've no idea, H.'

H was not in a good mood. He'd been on a new murder case for a week or so and really didn't need the distraction. The murder victim's head had been taken clean off. Hacked off with a saw. The body was a week old, but H was nowhere near an identification, and none of the recent missing persons cases checked out as possibilities. He needed to crack on with the case. But that now had to wait.

'What do you mean, you have no idea? You need to find out, pronto. We need to protect him.'

'H, you know how this works. His wife or someone he knows could have shopped him. We're not going to town on this one, he's not that important to us.'

'Nobody knows about his past. Just me, his wife, and you and your firm.'

'Really? He could have just as easily blabbed to someone. He likes a drink, doesn't he? People forget themselves when they've had a few. Anyway, how can you believe anything a man like that says? Nobody's sweating over this, just cut him loose H, just let things take their course.'

'Are you taking the piss? He worked for us. We owe him.'

But Jake Ardley was not kidding. He was cut from the same cloth as H, and was not about to be pressurised or backed-down.

'That's not how it works now, H. Pat O'Leary and his lot are yesterday's problem. Do you understand what I'm saying to you, DI Hawkins? Just drop it, there's nothing to be done. Drop it, it's ancient history now, and it's none of your fucking business anymore.'

\*\*\*

It was a frustratingly slow week; the days rolled by, with H fretting about the pregnancy and Pat O'Leary in equal measure. He arrived home from work on the Thursday after the wedding to find Julie sitting in the kitchen with Angela, who was watching Julie hard and holding a watch.

'What's happening, ladies?', said H, 'everything shipshape and Bristol fashion?'

Julie said nothing, but closed her eyes and took a deep breath.

'Yep, all in order,' said Angela. 'Julie's contractions are down to five minutes apart.'

'What does that tell us?' said H.

120

'It tells us, H, that her waters will be breaking soon, and that it's time to be getting her to the hospital.'

Julie was all matter-of-fact efficiency as she stood up slowly, holding the small of her back, collected her bag and let Angela help put on her coat. H felt a surge of excitement and anxiety rush him – he'd waited a long time for fatherhood, now he was almost there. He took Julie's bag, opened the front door for her, took her out into the murky London early-evening and eased her into the car.

Three hours later, sitting alone in a waiting room in Guy's Hospital, he was approached by a midwife. She informed him that things had 'slowed down', and that soon, given his wife's age, they would be making attempts to 'move things on.' He did with this information what he could, thanked the midwife, headed out into the corridor and barrelled towards the drinks machine in search of sweet tea.

He returned to the waiting room with his spoils, and was just beginning the process of engaging with his tasteless drink when a dishevelled and agitated Smethurst burst in.

'H, I've been looking for you everywhere.'

'Well, now you've found me. You're like a bad fucking penny son, always turning up at the wrong moment.'

'It's your mate, O'Leary, they've taken him.'

'Fuck-all I can do about it now.'

'You can, I think I know where he is. I've been keeping my ears to the ground since this all kicked off last week. I think they've got him in a safe house in Stockwell.'

'How do you know all this? You've come up with some good stuff in the past, I'll give you that, but knowledge of IRA safe houses? I don't fucking think so.'

'H, listen. I can't tell you how I know. But it's a very solid source. O'Leary might still be alive, they might want to interrogate him before they top him off. There's still a chance.'

'Then call the Old Bill.'

'What?'

'Dial 999 – you must have heard of it.'

'H, you know I don't do that. Anyway they'll think it's a crank call, or just send a couple of plodders out. By the time they do anything, if they do anything, he'll be dead.'

'Listen, I have to let this go. Just do what I told you and don't creep up on me again at a birth, a wedding, a funeral or any other fucking thing for that matter.'

'But H, I thought...'

'Well, now you know different,' said H. 'Now fuck off.'

\*\*\*

A week after the birth of Little Ronnie Hawkins, Old Father Thames gave up one of his periodic gruesome secrets. A badly decomposed, headless body was found by a treasure hunter on the southern bank, in Woolwich. H, who had asked to be alerted to any such eventuality as a matter of priority, was the first senior officer on the scene and took charge of the situation. He supervised the unwrapping of the layers of plastic sheeting the body had been bound in, and saw as soon as it was revealed that this was his man.'

'Jesus,' said PC Kyle Baker, who was first on the scene and sealed the area as soon as he knew it wasn't a crank call. Barker reeled back in shock and vomited as soon as he smelt, and saw, the contents of the package as it was unveiled. 'Steady on son,' said H, 'you'll get used to it.' He gave the boy a hit off his flask, checked he was OK, and started barking instructions here and there to his underlings and the ambulance crew before making for his car.

'Is that it?' said PC Barker, 'aren't you going to have a closer look at the rest of the body?'

'No need,' said H, 'I've got a pretty good idea of who it is, and how he died.'

H was already at the morgue when the body arrived, and got quickly into his groove, using the full force of his personality and clout to silence the doubts anyone around him might have had as he broke every procedural rule in the book – starting with fingerprinting the carcass himself and taking it from there.

When he returned to Scotland Yard he had the fingerprints run through the system, confirmed the identification and opened the case file for the murder of one Padraig Michael O'Leary.

'Head hacked clean off?' said his fellow DI, Helen Stone, chatting to H over coffee shortly after he set the murder investigation in motion. 'Not the IRA's usual modus operandi.'

'No,' said H, 'not their usual thing at all – they normally just put a bullet in the nut and dig a deep grave nobody finds for ten years. Maybe they were in a hurry, or O'Leary fought back. We'll probably never know.'

'Anything from forensics you can get your teeth into?'

'Not much – he was sealed in tight, by people who knew what they were doing,' said H.

'Doesn't really fit with the "they may have been in a hurry" hypothesis.'

'No, nothing about this is making much sense yet.'

'Looks like you've caught an absolute bastard on this one, H.'

'Yeah,' said H, 'you can say that again.'

***

Pat O'Leary never had a lot of friends, but there were a few people from some of the pubs he frequented over the years, and a few family members made the trip over from Ireland. H saw Smethurst lurking about at the margins, pale and indistinct, like he was a ghost himself, but otherwise recognised nobody.

The funeral procession turned up. The wife and son got out of their car, she looking haggard and careworn, he looking dazed and confused, like a rabbit caught in headlights. The undertakers went through their paces with their usual deference for the dead. The coffin was taken into the crematorium, the twenty or so guests filed in behind.

Hither Green crematorium in Lewisham, opened in the middle of the Victorian period, came with grand ornamental entrance gates and two Gothic chapels. A large terraced area was added after the second world war, to commemorate the death of six teachers and thirty-eight children who died when their school was bombed. The ornamental gates had long gone but the cremations rolled on, back to back, each one passing through the conveyor belt of death with mechanical efficiency.

The service was short. A couple of hymns. A few Irish folk songs. A eulogy delivered by a priest nobody in the congregation had ever met – O'Leary hadn't visited a church in all his years in England. Outside, such flowers as there were had already begun to wilt. H approached O'Leary's estranged wife, Nancy, to offer his condolences. She was not in the mood to receive them.

'I have nothing to say to you,' she said. 'Please leave.'

'I just wanted…'

'I don't care what you want. This is your fault. You got him tangled up in all this. You used him, and when he was of no use you abandoned him. Just go, now.'

H was lost for words. He wanted to explain. He wanted to try and make her feel better. But he couldn't. 'I'm sorry,' he said, and turned on his heel, and left.

Relieved to be alone again, and in his car, H drove directly to a quiet country pub outside Deal. He pulled into the pub car park, killed the sound of Sammy Davis singing *It Ain't*

*Necessarily So*, waved to a man sitting behind one of the windows drinking a pint of Guinness, took an envelope from the glove compartment and headed inside. He got a pint of his own at the bar and sat at the window table.

'Hello H, how'd it all go? Full of tears and woe, were they all?'

'Some of them were, Pat, yes, some of them were.'

'Well, it's not every day a man gets a fresh report on his own funeral.'

'You really want the details, Pat, or shall we just get down to business?'

'OK, spare me the details H – I have no wish to know how few people attended the occasion.'

H handed O'Leary the thickly-packed envelope, which was received with a silent nod.

'Cheers then, H.' said O'Leary, raising his glass, 'here's to old friends. And to absent ones.'

'Cheers Pat, good health.'

O'Leary checked the contents of the envelope, smiled broadly, and said 'So how you going to deal with the matter of my murder then H? It's bound to damage your reputation for high clear-up rates.'

'Not your problem,' said H. 'Your problem is getting down to Dover, slipping out of the country and living a long and happy life. Mind you, no one's looking for you now, so you're a dot on the card to get away with it if you're sensible.'

'Thanks H, you're an absolute diamond, if there's anything I can ever do for you.'

'Best thing you can do for me mate is live well, wherever you go, and never show your face in London again.'

'Don't plan to H. I'm heading for…'

'No, don't tell me. I'd keep that on a need-to-know basis if I were you. And I don't need to know. Just get as far away from here as you can, and hope your friends from the Emerald Isle never find out you're still alive.'

'Does anyone else know, about all this?'

'You, me and Ronnie Ruddock. He said to say hello, and to tell you to make sure you spend the sixty grand he put in that envelope wisely.'

'Who wound Smethurst up and set him going about me being taken by the Provos?'

'John Viney – you remember him. I just asked him to start a rumour. He doesn't know why. The grapevine did the rest.'

'H, I don't know how to thank you. You've taken a huge risk for me. If anyone finds out what you did, with your headless friend and all.'

'Well, that's my problem, Pat. I look after my own, and I deal with the consequences.'

'You're a grand man to have as a friend, H. One other thing's been bothering me though – how were you so sure my dead body, so to speak, would wash up?'

'I wasn't. But the old boy father Thames usually gives up his secrets, sooner or later. I just had to hope it'd be sooner. And it all had to look real, not contrived. There's some clever coppers about, you know.'

Pat O'Leary nodded his assent to this, and smiled again. The two men finished their drinks, left the pub, and walked in silence into the car park. O'Leary stopped at a battered old Ford Mondeo and said, 'This is me, H.' H held out his hand for the final shake, but O'Leary pulled him closer and hugged him tight, patting him hard on the back.

'There is one thing,' said H, as O'Leary pulled open the car door.

'What, H, anything.'

'Your missus, she hates me. If the pull of home ever gets too much and you find yourself back here one day, or you ever write to her, just tell her…'

'Tell her what, H?'

'Nothing, forget it,' said H. 'Good sailing, Pat. Stay lucky.'

O'Leary climbed into his car, fired up the engine and H watched him pull away in the direction of Dover. He went back to his own car, his thoughts returning now to his own priorities. He had a new son to think about, and a new case to pretend to conduct and close. His biggest regret in the whole sorry mess was the dead man who would never now find justice. Nabbing a dead body from the morgue and passing him off as O'Leary had been surprising easy. But it meant a murdered person, even one of no fixed abode who nobody seemed to have missed or cared about, wouldn't ever be identified, would never get justice. But the ruined carcass of one man had helped prevent the murder of another. Such was life, thought H. And such was death.

He remained in his car seat for a while, reflecting on the last couple of weeks, before closing the door and pulling out his phone. He called home, planning to give it just a couple of rings so as not to wake up anyone who might be sleeping, but Julie answered it straight away.

'Hello babes,' said H. 'I'm on my way back now, all done for the day. How are you?'

'Oh, I'm fine, H,' Julie said woozily. 'Just fine.'

'And how's Little Ronnie?'

'He's fine as well, he's just perfect. He's sleeping at the moment. Sleeping like a baby.'

# Unsafe Space

# November 2017

'H, you need to see this babes,' shouted Olivia. 'Quick, or you'll miss it.' H heard her, loud and clear; he put the kettle back down and bustled along the passage to the living room, where Olivia was watching the TV news.

'What is it? What's happened?' said H.

'Just watch it. It's on a loop.'

H sat down on the sofa and focused on the screen. He saw what looked like a massive street demonstration in the West End, a huge mass of people snaking around Parliament Square, along Whitehall and up to Trafalgar Square. There were colourful banners and placards as far as the eye could see, with all the usual suspects represented.

'What, Liv? So the soap dodgers are having a march. You've seen one, you've seen them all. What's so important that I had to run here halfway through making a cup of tea?'

'Just watch, it's coming up.'

H did as he was told, Olivia never having been one for wasting his time.

H watched as the camera moved in through the thick of the crowd and arrived at a crash barrier, the other side of which was heavily lined by police. It was the stretch of Whitehall, on the other side of the Cenotaph from Downing Street, that was home to a couple of statues that H always made Olivia stop and study with him when they were uptown, playing tourist. One was of Field Marshall the Viscount Slim, and just along from it his favourite, apart from the Churchill statue in Parliament Square itself, of Field Marshall Lord Montgomery, the war hero shot through the right lung at the Battle of Ypres, only to return to the fray at Passchendaele.

H exploded out of his chair in a rage, a rage no less hair-raising to Olivia for its being entirely predictable.

'What the fuck! What have they done to Monty?'

'Well, H, they've…'

'Fucking hell, Liv, have a look at that. What have these soap-dodgers done to Monty?'

'H, why don't you sit down babes? You remember what the doctor said. Sit yourself down babes…please. I'll finish the tea.'

By the time H returned himself to the sofa, and had taken a deep breath, the image of Monty had gone and the story moved on to something about the Great British Bake-off. His heart was pounding and there were little stabbing pains shooting around his chest. He stayed put and continued his deep breathing; he'd finally learned, after long and bitter experience and Olivia's persistent pleading, to listen to his doctor.

'Babes, bring the tablet with you when you come back, will you? We'll need to have another look at it on Youtube or something.'

Olivia was already on her way, with a tray containing a plate of chocolate biscuits and two teas. The tablet she had tucked under her arm.

She set the tray down on the coffee table, and said 'OK my love, we'll have a look – if you promise me you'll stay sitting down and focus on your breathing.'

'Promise.'

Olivia opened up Twitter, found a collection of photographs of the desecrated statue and placed it on the coffee table for her husband to examine. The upper part of Monty's figure had borne the brunt of it, having received the attentions of someone with corrosives, paint and, by the look of it, a blowtorch. They had tried to melt the bronze statue with fire. There was no way of telling how structural the damage was, but Monty was not looking good. His face had been scoured and coloured with red and yellow paint. H took this in, sitting down and exercising all the self- control

131

he could, but when they reached a photo of the torso section of the statue and saw a huge swastika painted on it in white, Olivia decided it was time to pause the session and talk things through before her husband chewed all the way through his cheek and spattered her new sofa with blood and gristle.

'Disrespectful little bastards,' she said quietly.

'Yep,' said H 'disrespectful, and ungrateful, and absolutely clueless. Do these spoilt little brats even know who Monty was? Do they know that if it weren't for him and Churchill they'd be goose-stepping up and down Whitehall being reviewed by some German general on a platform? Don't they understand anything? Don't they know anything?'

'I don't know, love. Maybe they're just following the fashion.'

'What fashion?'

'For vandalizing and pulling old statues down. Amisha told me about it. These student types have got a fashion for destroying things they don't like. There's been a lot of it going on in America. I suppose it's caught on here now.'

'God give me strength. I just don't get it Liv. What are the schools teaching them? What do their parents tell them?'

Olivia shrugged, and smiled, trying to change H's mood.

He took a deep breath, and smiled back.

'I just don't understand it. Anyway, did you know Monty was born in Kennington, Liv? South London man, he was.'

'Yes, you may have mentioned that on one or two of our visits uptown.'

'Well, I'm proud of him. We were all proud of him, once. People used to love Monty.'

'Yes babes. Here, drink your tea before it gets cold.'

'No, I don't fancy it now babes, thanks. I think I'll just get my head down. All this self-control has knocked the bollocks out of me. I'd have been better off just going garrity like I used to.'

'Alright love, I'll be up in a bit. Have a good night's sleep – you'll feel better in the morning.'

***

But H did not feel better in the morning. He rose early, got into his training gear and went for his usual jog around Avery Hill Park. He ran for three or four minutes and then slowed down, again as usual, to his power walk, and then down again to his casual stroll. But none of these exertions cleared his head, as he hoped they might. His mind was troubled by something he couldn't quite put his finger on. He was personally upset by yesterday's outrage, but something else was gnawing at him.

He told Olivia that he didn't understand the people who'd damaged the statue, what their motivations were. He knew things had been changing, but think as he might he could not come to terms with why, or how, Lord Field Marshall Montgomery had wound up with a swastika, of all things, emblazoned on his chest. It just didn't make any sense. At all. It was this that really troubled him.

He needed answers. He'd come across plenty of PC-programmed types in the course of his work – he saw a flashing vision of his friend Graham Miller-Marchant and his jargon-filled presentations for the murder squad at the Yard, in the days before H straightened him out – and tried to remember their buzzwords and catchphrases and silly ideas. But he came up more or less blank; none of it had ever sunk in, perhaps because he'd never been listening.

He left the park and picked up his walking pace a little as he headed for home, feeling better now that he'd decided to talk to someone. He had Amisha, his former colleague and friend, who knew a lot about that sort of thing, and he could even talk to dopey Justin, the sociology lecturer who'd stolen his first wife off him. It had taken several years, but he was getting along cordially enough with him these days. He'd know; he'd know everything.

Energised now, H broke into a full-tilt run five hundred yards out, so as to arrive looking hot and sweaty for Olivia's benefit. He burst through the door full of vim and vigour, headed straight for the kitchen, and swept Olivia up into his arms for a kiss.

'Good run?' she said.

'Yep, blinding. Absolutely blinding, my lovely. Any danger of a bit of egg and bacon?'

'No, not on a Monday morning. You know the rules. You can have some porridge, and a bit of toast. I'll put the kettle on. And before I forget, you had a call, about work. Someone in Tonbridge wants to know if you'll look into something for him. Said he didn't want to talk details over the phone, could you go down there and see him. Sounded nice enough.'

'Right you are, doll,' said H, collapsing into a chair. 'I'll give them a bell after breakfast.'

***

H drove down to Tonbridge soon after breakfast, having been assured by a Mr. Anthony Phillipson that his expenses would be covered. Mr. Phillipson had sounded like a modest, gentle and cultured man with a lot on his mind, and when H pulled into the driveway of a solid detached house on the outskirts of the town his appearance fitted with H's snap assessment. He was waiting outside the house, obviously agitated – a rangy, well-dressed man in his early sixties with a dignified, self-possessed air.

H got out of the car and walked into a firm handshake and big smile. 'It's a pleasure to meet you, Mr. Hawkins,' said Phillipson. 'I followed your career with interest, over the years. I do hope you can help us.'

134

'I'll do my best, Mr. Phillipson, you can rest assured on that score. If I take the case.'

'Good. Please come inside. Rosalyn has made tea.'

H was led into a sitting room containing a three-piece suite in a floral design, a coffee table set between the sofa and chairs, and a small, svelte looking woman sitting at it pouring tea. 'Ah, good of you to come Mr. Hawkins,' she said, rising. 'Will you have tea?'

'I've never been known to say no to a cup of tea, Mrs. Phillipson. Thank you. Two sugars please.'

'Right you are, do sit yourself down.'

The three of them settled into the furniture.

'How can I help?' said H.

The Phillipsons looked at one another uneasily, as if each of them wanted the other to get the ball rolling. Mr. Phillipson took it on. 'Well, it's a difficult situation. And a strange one, I...'

'Mr. P,' said H, 'Let me stop you there. I've spent a very long time dealing with difficult situations. That's what I do. Please don't worry about what I might think. I can see you're both upset about something. Just tell me what it is. Start from the beginning, like you're telling me a story. Give me facts.'

'OK, the matter concerns our son. He's been injured, and suffered an injustice, and I'd like you to help us set the record straight and make someone culpable for what's happened to him.'

'Go on,' said H. 'What injury, what injustice?'

'Well, about a month ago he was beaten up at his university. He was attacked by a gang of thugs and suffered a shattered cheekbone, and concussion. The injuries were inflicted with a baseball bat. He's been very shaken by the whole thing, and...'

'Let's stay focused, Mr. P. Your son has taken a hiding? Very sorry to hear that. Where does the injustice you mention come in?'

'Not one of his attackers has been identified. The university authorities haven't even launched an investigation of any sort. We tried to involve the police, but the university just batted them away, told them nothing had happened on their premises. And the worst thing is, that Martin got the blame for the whole thing. The university has thrown him out.'

'On what basis?' said H.

'Some kind of trumped up disciplinary thing. They say he violated their code of conduct, he's a racist and they are within their rights to exclude him. We have a lawyer looking into that, but what we really want is...'

Mrs. Phillipson sighed, heavily. 'What we want, Mr. Hawkins, is to get to the bottom of this damn mess. Here is a fact for you. Martin says one of the lecturers is behind the whole thing. He says she put the mob up to beat him, that she covered up for them, and that she arranged to have him removed from the university.'

'Something is rotten in that place, Mr. Hawkins,' continued Mr. Phillipson. 'It's not like a university at all, not as Rosalyn and I knew them. It's more like some sort of weird cult.'

'Which university are we talking about?' said H.

'Naismiths College – you know, in Lewisham,' said Mrs. Green.

'I do,' said H. 'It's on my old patch. And what was he studying?'

'Sociology,' said Mr. Phillipson. 'Not the subject we'd have chosen for him. We saw him as going more towards law, or perhaps medicine. But we had a lot of trouble with him when he was a lad, he went off the rails for a bit. In the end we were just happy he wanted to go to university at all.'

'And it's not just a matter of wanting justice done,' said Mrs. Phillipson, with tears beginning to well in her eyes. 'We've had to work so hard to get Martin on the straight and narrow, you know, on some normal sort of track, and he's our only child, and what is he to make of all this? He's staying with a friend in London at the moment, mulling it all over.'

'OK, I've got the broad picture. I propose you knock up another pot of tea, and then we'll get down to the details. That's where the devil always is. I want to know about the circumstances of the beating, and I want to know more about this sociology lecturer.'

***

'Well, as to the circumstances,' said Mr. Phillipson as his wife brought in the fresh pot, 'this is where it gets really strange. Like some macabre comedy. Frankly, we're a little worried you'll find it hard to take seriously.'

'Your boy has had his face smashed in with a baseball bat, Mr. P. That's all the serious I need. Go on.'

'Well, there was a fancy-dress party to celebrate something or other, and Martin went as Tommy Cooper – you know, the comedian.'

'Yes, Mr. P, I know Tommy Cooper. Funniest man who ever lived. Good to know the youngsters still like him.'

'I made sure Martin knew some of the old stars, but I doubt many of his peers would know Tommy.'

'OK, so he's gone to a party dressed as Tommy Cooper,' said H.

'Yes, in a big bulky suit, big shoes and, of course the fez. And his hair all messed up. He looked hilarious, in the photos.'

'And?'

'And at some point during the party he was asked, by a delegation led by Poppy Stackridge, to remove the fez.'

'Why?' said H.

'Well, this is where it all starts to get very peculiar, and difficult to understand. It seems they've developed a whole new language, you see, which it seems necessary to know, and use, to participate in the life of the college. And also, in our case, to try and figure out what's happened.'

'I'm not getting it, Mr. P. Why was he asked to take the fez off?' said H.

'Because,' said Mr. Phillipson, shaking his head, 'Stackridge said it was wrong to wear the dress of someone from a different culture. She called it "Cultural appropriation".'

'Cultural what?' said H. 'It's just a fez? A Tommy Cooper fez,' said H.

'Well,' said Mr. Phillipson, with his head in his hands. 'Apparently Stackridge contends that it's all connected to colonialism, the suppression of other cultures.'

'Have they got rules for this 'cultural appropriation', at Naismiths?'

'Apparently. Well, they've got speech codes, which are sort of formal I think. And now it seems they also have a sort of informal dress code. But the rules are not clear. They're making it all up as they go along,' said Mr. Phillipson.

'So did your boy remove the fez, as requested?'

'No, he did not. He's been raised to stand up for himself,' said Mrs. Phillipson. 'so he told them to get lost, and that the fez would be staying.'

'What happened next?'

'He stayed at the party, in the fez, while the rest of them froze him out. I understand he did a few Tommy Cooper impersonations, he's talented like that, but a certain group would not fraternize with him, and shouted him down. They wore him out, so he left early, alone, and was confronted by a group of thugs in the car park, who removed his fez and beat him up. That is what happened, Mr. Hawkins,' said Mr. Phillipson.

'Did he recognise any of his assailants?'

'No, they were masked-up, and said nothing. They just took the fez, knocked him to the ground and administered the beating. But...'

'I know, Mr. P. It was too much of a coincidence. What about this Poppy Stackridge. How sure is Martin that she was behind it?'

'He's certain. Martin says she's a very powerful personality, and runs the department like her own little fiefdom. She indoctrinates the students with her way of thinking, and winds them up like little radicals to go out on demonstrations and conduct all sorts of "activism". Martin says sessions on "revolutionary violence" and "militant resistance" are her bread and butter. She's at it all the time.'

'So Martin thinks she got her paper revolutionaries to dish out the beating, and then got him chucked out as a troublemaker to cover for it.'

'Precisely,' said Mrs. Phillipson. 'Violence first, manipulation of the "rules" second. She's wrecked his educational career.'

'Right,' said H, 'got it. So what you need is a case built against Stackridge, for me to present sufficient evidence for your lawyer to take the college to the cleaners. Yes?'

'Yes,' said Mr. Phillipson. 'We want Martin readmitted, and Stackridge out of her job; and we intend to sue Naismiths College for every penny its worth. To make the point. Can you help us?'

'Absolutely. Leave it with me, I'll get onto it straight away.' H stood, and shook the Phillipsons' hands. 'You'd better give me the address your boy is staying at. I'll be in touch as soon as we've got something to sink our teeth into.'

H was as good as his word, and decided to head for Lewisham straight away. He wanted to have a good poke about and size the place up as soon as possible. He knew a couple of the porters at Naismiths from the old days, and thought they might be able to get him situated without anyone paying too much attention. He didn't suppose the university would be particularly pleased to see him on their patch.

First order of business, though, was to pick Justin's brains. Justin was the only academic he knew. H recalled that he used to describe himself as a 'radical criminologist', which sounded close enough to sociology to be useful. H wanted a little more information, and a grounding in the thing he was about to walk into. The Phillipsons had given him a start, but he needed more.

He settled into a groove on the A23 and punched Justin's number into the hands-free set. Justin answered the call straight away. 'Hello H,' he said, 'to what do I owe this unexpected pleasure?'

'Listen, mate – I'm on a job. I need some background info on the people I'm looking at. You got a minute?'

'Yep. Ten, in fact. I'm between lectures.'

'Good man. OK, in a nutshell I've got a thing to look into at Naismiths College. What I want to know is all this "cultural appropriation" and such like…is all that your game?'

'No, not really H.'

'I thought you were a full-on lefty?'

'I am, but you're talking about all this new stuff, which I think is just emotion-driven. Spoiled brats wanting to be victims, and wanting to tear down anything they don't agree with. I do believe in reforming the system. But I also believe in debating the facts and then making reforms. That's the main thing. I believe in facts, like you do.'

'What d'you mean? Everyone believes in facts, don't they? Except nutters?'

'Well, maybe some of these people are borderline nutters. You know, the Social Justice Warrior types, and their teachers. The teachers most of all. The kids themselves are too young to know any better, and they're easy to indoctrinate.'

'What, like a brainwashing cult?'

'Yes, in places. I think it's easy to over-exaggerate all of this and think all the world is collapsing around us, like a *Daily Mail* headline, but some places are a touch extreme. Naismiths has a reputation for it…something of a hotbed.'

'Fuck me, sounds like a proper Mad Hatter's tea party. What should I expect in my dealings with them?'

'Well, don't expect them to listen to reason. Or have any. They're driven by emotion and ideology, so they won't be prepared to listen to you at all, once they know who you are. They'll call you a *Nazi* – they don't know what the word means, they just use it to describe everyone who disagrees with them. Then they'll shout you down, or retreat into their safe space.'

'What the fuck is a *safe space*?'

'A place where they have everything their own way, into which views other than their own are not allowed.'

'Sounds like a bunch of four-year olds, hiding under their blankets in the nursery.'

'Yep. Basically.'

'But capable of violence and serious criminal damage.'

'Oh yes, if they're wound up and set to work properly by one of their gurus.'

'These would be the kind of people who'd be out tearing down monuments?'

'Yes, spot on. Anything else I can help you with?'

'No, thanks mate, that's blinding. Things are beginning to fall into place. Cheers,' said H, moving his arm to end the call.

'One last thing, H,' Justin said. 'Be careful. These kids and their teachers are misguided, but they're not stupid, and they can be dangerous.'

'What are they going to do...spit their dummies into my face and blubber all over me?'

'No, they're going to film you, and record you, and goad you into saying something they can use against you, or dig something up from your past. No shortage of ammunition for them there, is there? They'll haul you all over the media until they've ruined your reputation.'

H laughed. 'Too late for that, 'he said, 'Joey Jupiter did that for me years ago.'

'Joey Jupiter was a rational seeker of truth. He's already old-school. This lot are irrational, full of hate and versed in all the dark arts of media manipulation. They'll come at you, once you start sniffing around. Make no mistake about it — they'll come at you.'

\*\*\*

H pulled into the Naismith College car park, took off the jacket and tie he'd worn for his interview with the Phillipsons, rolled up his sleeves and barrelled into the building the back way in search of Snowy Bedford, an old Bermondsey friend of fifty years. He found him in the porter's lodge, surreptitiously playing cards with two of his mates.

'Slow day, Snow?' said H, putting his head round the door. Snowy Bedford was so surprised he dropped a card on the floor, face-up, and the others saw it. End of game. 'Fuck me H, what you doing here? Has someone died?'

'No mate, I'm on a job. Can you do me a favour?'

142

'Name it mate.'

'Well, between us four I want to have a look at a sociology lecturer called Poppy Stackridge. Know of her?'

All of the porters laughed. 'Be hard not to,' said Snowy. 'She's always causing trouble about the place.'

'How do you mean?'

'Well, organizing protests and "emergency meetings", whipping up trouble every chance she gets. Causes us a lot of extra work.'

'Not a fan then?'

'Nah mate, she's a bit of a nightmare. Her students like her though – she's got quite a following.'

'Is she about today?'

Snowy checked the schedule on his screen. 'Yep, she's on at two o'clock. Main auditorium.'

'Can you get me in there?'

'What, you want permission to attend her lecture.'

'No, I want to go in, undercover.'

All three porters laughed.

'H, April Fool's day was ages ago. Have you got nothing better to do but come round here taking the piss? Have you lost the plot entirely since they slung you out the Met?'

'Mate, listen to me. I ain't got all day. I'm on a job for a client, and this woman is important to the case. I want to have a look at her, see what she's like, how she deals with her students, that sort of thing. I want to get in there, unobtrusive like.'

'What, as a mature student?'

The gale of uproarious laughter that now came from the porter's lodge turned heads; people in the corridor were stopping to see what the fuss was all about.

H closed the door and said through clenched teeth: 'What did I say about wanting to be unobtrusive? Will you all stop fucking about. This is serious.'

More laughter. Snowy's eyes looked like they were on stalks as he stared at H in continuing disbelief. 'Tell me you're fucking kidding me.'

'Look,' said another member of the card school, 'out of the window, there's a pig flying.' More laugher, and now H couldn't help himself, and cracked a smile.

'Listen you fuckers, I'm serious. Snow, I want to go in as one of your lot. Borrow a blazer and fiddle about at the back of the auditorium on an emergency maintenance problem. Something like that. Can it be done, or not?'

'Of course it can H. No problem, old son,' said Snow, starting to realise H actually meant it. Me and you can creep in there a quarter of an hour before it starts, and get up top and open a couple of panels in the back wall, keep our heads down. I'll book it into the system now as an emergency. How'd you fancy "heating system malfunction"?'

*\*\*\**

H and Snowy pottered about quietly at the back of the auditorium, ignored by the forty or so students who filed in, occupied the first three rows of seats and sat looking into their phones. There was not much interaction between individuals, and a soporific calm prevailed. These kids didn't look much like the kill-'em'-and-eat-'em warriors of Justin's description. But this changed when, on the stroke of two o'clock, the diminutive form of Poppy Stackridge burst in through the door at the front of the room, strode purposely towards the lecture pulpit, turned full-front to face her audience and silently raised her right arm in a clenched fist. Her followers stood up and did the same, some emitting whoops and hollers of various kinds, and the air began to crackle with energy and purpose.

'Game on,' whispered H to Snowy. 'What the fuck have we stumbled into here?'

Poppy Stackridge cleared her throat, adjusted her black-rimmed spectacles, put her hands on her hips, and began to speak in a sort of accelerated version of the old Oxbridge drawl.

'OK people: to business. I'll begin with my lecture, as usual. It'll be a little shorter than usual, on "Intersectionality and Feminist Praxis".'

H looked at Snowy. Snowy looked at H. Both shook their heads in a gesture that said *no, me neither.*

'And after that,' Stackridge continued, 'we'll bring in the talking stick and get into our thoughts and feelings about what we all experienced yesterday.' This announcement, whatever it might portend, was greeted with further whoops of glee from the students.

Snowy hunkered down still lower behind the back row of seats. 'What the fuck is a *talking stick*?' he whispered.

'Fucked if I know, Snow,' replied H. 'But I know one thing – Martin Phillipson is well out of all this bollocks.'

\*\*\*

Poppy Stackridge began her lecture. H stood up quietly and pretended, with his back to the stage, to fiddle with a valve. He wanted to hide in plain sight, and make sure she saw him. She paid him no mind whatsoever, and he got back down onto his haunches, switched on his phone's voice recorder, and pulled out his notebook.

His plan was to make notes of keywords and phrases in the lecture for later clarification by Justin and Amisha. All crimes, he'd long ago learnt, had a motivation, and he wanted to understand what motivated Martin's beating. He was expecting the going to be tough, but Stackridge exceeded all his expectations. In a steady, one-pitch drone she proceeded to give a talk so full of jargon and twisted, made-up logic, that H might as well have been listening to a foreign language. He could gain no purchase on the overall sense of what she was saying, and fell to jotting down words she repeated a lot that seemed to be of significance. He noted that "Intersectionality", "Cisgender" and 'Microaggression" cropped up most frequently.

He wrote them down.

In the short pauses between sentences he scanned about and noticed that the students were sitting in rapt silence. He popped his head above the chairs and saw that they were sitting bolt upright, their fingers flowing silently across the keypads of their laptops, tablets and phones, hanging on every word.

'I'll give her this much, Snow: she's got them well motivated, and well drilled. They're absolutely eating out of her hand, whatever it is she's feeding them.'

But Snowy was out for the count, stretched out on the floor with his hands behind his head. This was clearly not his cup of tea and, H surmised, he probably had a hangover to sleep off.

H waited it out, losing his focus and letting his mind drift. He thought about the homes these students might have come from, and the fact that their parents were paying – as the Phillipsons had informed him – nine grand a year for this, double that and more if they were from abroad. Were they all from such good, solid homes, cherished by loving, hard-working parents who did everything they could to provide the best for them? He supposed they must be.

He thought about his own children. Ronnie, a couple of years older than most of these, had already earned a double-PhD from the university of life and was his own man; Grace, on the other side of the world, still ignoring his phone calls and emails, had her own thriving beauty salon, he knew with satisfaction; and Little Harry, well he had a long way to go yet, but his father would be doing everything he could to get him into a trade, or the armed forces, or anything real and useful. Anything but this, at nine grand a year.

His ruminations were interrupted by a burst of applause, the usual hooting and hollering, and a cascade of upward movement and fist-clenching.

'OK,' said Stackridge, 'essays, reviews and strategy brainstorms due as per the schedule. Now, its circle time. Toby, let's get this plinth out of the way.'

'Wake up, Snow,' H whispered excitedly, 'I think it's time for the *talking stick*.'

\*\*\*

Toby, a hulking figure of about six feet two inches, sporting a nose ring and shoulder-length blond hair, did as he was told. The group formed itself into a circle at the now-spacious front of the auditorium; Poppy Stackridge placed herself in the centre of it, holding with both hands a carved stick almost as tall as herself.

She banged the stick on the ground, hard, three times and said 'I will fight the patriarchy until my dying breath. Yesterday we took a great leap forward, with a massive display of intersectional unity. The future is ours. This is my truth.'

Toby – he seemed to be featuring heavily in proceedings – stood up, walked to the centre of the circle and took the stick. Poppy Stackridge sat in the spot he vacated. 'I will fight the patriarchy until my dying breath,' he said. 'Male privilege is my shame and my struggle. In this struggle I will prevail. The future is ours. This is my truth.'

At this the group exploded into applause, with shouts of affirmation and encouragement, until the students and Poppy Stackridge could contain themselves no more. They rose as one to their feet and began to flail about in what looked like a tribal rain dance, whooping and thrashing around like dervishes. After a time a chant emerged from the chaos:

*Said hey, said ho, masculinity's got to go.*
*Said hey, said ho, masculinity's got to go.*

'This lot are absolutely fucking barking mad H. Have you ever seen anything like this?' said Snowy.

'No, I ain't mate. And I don't want to see a lot more. I've had a bellyful. Why don't you creep out the back door and make yourself scarce. No need for anything to blow back on you. I'm going to break the party up now.'

'Right you are mate, swing by and let us know how you got on before you go.'

'Will do, Snow, if I get the chance. Cheers.'

Snowy left. H gathered up his bits and pieces, and walked slowly down the stairs towards where all the action was. Poppy Stackridge noticed him when he was about half way down. She took the stick and beat the ground with it, and raised her hand. The students fell silent as H reached the bottom of the stairs, and formed themselves into a clustered semicircle. H stood to face them.

'OK, Your Ladyship,' he said, addressing Stackridge. 'All done. Should be lovely and warm in a bit. Give it about ten minutes.'

She glowered at him over her black rims, but said nothing. She stepped forward a pace or two. Her followers followed her.

'You're welcome,' said H. 'Before I go, though, I couldn't help but overhear what you were saying while I was working. Very interesting. Do you mind if I ask you to clarify one or two points for me? I'm only a humble porter, I know, but some of us working class types do like to at least try and keep up with things.' He fished out the notebook from the blazer he was wearing, biting down on the laughter that was beginning to bubble up from his stomach.

'So, if I may...'

But Poppy Stackridge still said nothing; she was alternating between looking searchingly into H's face, and swiping and scrolling around in her phone.

'As I was saying, I just have one or two points. To start with, I'm not entirely clear on "microaggression". Is it...'

'You just committed one when you called the professor "Your Ladyship". Textbook microaggression, born of male privilege,' snarled an acned girl got up as a skinhead, high-leg, Cherry Red Doctor Martens boots and all. 'I think it's time for you to leave.' The group agreed, and began to inch towards him as one. Poppy Stackridge still said nothing, but simply raised her free hand to halt them, continuing to work the phone with the other.

'OK, that clears that one up – thank you,' said H. 'That really just leaves "Intersectionality" and...'

H was enjoying himself; he'd have been happy playing this game all day. But suddenly the mood changed. 'Got you, you fascist bastard,' screamed Poppy Stackridge at the top of her lungs, punching the air in exultation. 'I knew it. I never forget a face.' She turned to face the group and displayed her phone, which now had a full-screen mugshot of H on it, for all to see.

'People,' she shouted, 'meet the Detective Inspector Harry Hawkins. This is the bastard Joey Jupiter tried to bring down a few years back. Maybe we'll have more success.' She turned to H, and addressed him directly for the first time.

'What the hell are you doing here?'

'Well, as you may know I am no longer with the Metropolitan Police. I'm a porter now. A man's gotta do what a man's gotta do.'

'Porter my arse! You're a private detective. What are you doing here? Who are you working for?'

'Well, that's for me to know, and you to find out,' said H.

'OK. Time for you to leave. Toby, escort this fascist primate off the premises, will you please?'

Toby stepped forward, and got into H's face. 'Out! Now!' he said.

H stood his ground and put his hands in his pockets, trying hard not to break into laughter.

'Now! Or else I'll...' said Toby, who had a voice reminiscent of Prince Charles, now H came to think of it.

'Are you threatening me, spindle?' said H with a smirk. Forty phone cameras captured it.

Toby held his ground, but looked at Poppy Stackridge, hoping for some signal as to what to do next.

'Of course he isn't, Mr. Hawkins. We'd simply like you to leave now. You have no right or authority to be here. Time to go.'

He hadn't been wrong about the Mad Hatter's tea party aspect of it all. The world was turned upside down: he was now a fascist, and these kids, and whichever morons had daubed the swastika on Monty's chest, were the good guys.

They started chanting, their banked faces contorted with hate.

H felt like he was in some surreal Bolshevik pre-school playgroup. It was too much. He began to laugh, with a free, open laughter that enraged them further.

He stood, facing the mob, tuned them out and reflected on the experience as they raged: plum-toned people called Poppy and Toby were getting on his case about his 'privilege' – him, a Bermondsey boy, son of a tipper lorry driver, refugee from the education system at the age of sixteen, war fighter, low-paid copper at the sharp end of his society's moral chaos...some privilege that had all been. This was just about the most absurd situation he'd been in in his life, and all his instincts and body processes were telling him to bitch slap Toby up and down the corridor for ten minutes and spit a torrent of robust home truths into the face of Poppy Stackridge.

150

But that was what they wanted. Justin was right. If Poppy Stackridge and her sheep filmed him doing the things he felt like doing his freedom could quickly become a thing of the past. He reined himself in, and bit his tongue, and suddenly understood everything. These little bastards were holding all the trump cards. They were getting things their own way – they'd shut him up. Even him. He wasn't cowed, in any way, but they'd shut him up and cobbled him.

There was nothing for it: he'd have to leave. They'd film it, and splash it all over the Internet, and make it look like a humiliating defeat, but he needed to get out before something worse even than that happened. He turned sharply on his heels, and walked slowly away. The students formed immediately into an air-punching marching escort, following him along the corridors and towards the exit. All of them with their phones held high, recording, recording everything.

H reached the exit door, and just as he crossed it Toby pushed him hard in the middle of the back, so that he spilled out of the building and onto his front, like a circus clown. H, who had in his time crushed the windpipes of infinitely harder men than Toby for less, stayed down for a few seconds and struggled to regain his composure. He could hear the chanting and cheering of the students behind him, but more clearly, he could hear, in his mind, the yet-to-be-spoken words that his enemies, and probably some of his friends, would soon be taunting him with: *the great Harry Hawkins, scourge of the criminal classes, chased out of a university, thrown out by a soap-dodging bedwetter. How the mighty fall.*

\*\*\*

Snowy Bedford leaned down and helped him to his feet, and they walked together to H's car.

'Well, that went well,' said Snowy.

'Yeah. I think I might have blotted my copybook here, Snow. What do you reckon? Think they'll have me back?'

Snowy laughed. H clambered into his car and, as he wrestled with the seatbelt, Snowy leaned in and whispered 'Don't worry mate, me and the boys will take care of the little prick who pushed you. We'll let things settle down for a bit, and…'

'Nah, you're alright Snow. He's just a clueless little boy. Doesn't know his arse from his elbow; she's just manipulating the shit out of him. It's not worth the effort. No harm done.'

'No harm done? H, he made you look like a wanker, and all on video. Are you…'

'No, seriously, Snow. Leave him be. He's just one of the little oily rags – I'm after the engineer.'

'OK, if you say so mate, but the Harry Hawkins I knew…'

'Would have done the same,' said H. 'Say what you like about me, Snow, but I've never been a bully, and I'm not about to start having misguided little kids done over.' He sparked up the engine, said 'Alright then mate, cheers. See you soon, give my love to Sue,' and pulled out of the car park to join the usual snarling traffic on the one-way system, heading south.

He settled into the traffic flow, such as it was, and punched Sinatra's *Sings for Only the Lonely* into the music system to calm him down. It was one of his favourite albums and, though there was a lot of emotional turmoil on it, the beautiful melodies and Frank at the peak of his game usually made him feel much better.

He needed to get home and talk to Olivia. The fun and games at Naismiths, while hardly registering on the trauma-scale of his life and career as a whole, had left him agitated. He was not looking forward much to the stick he'd be getting once everyone saw the images, but that was not what was really eating at him. It was the sheer ignorance of the kids he'd seen, and the ruthless way Stackridge was manipulating and moulding them.

Frank and Nelson Riddle, who arranged the album, worked their magic. H began to relax, and get some perspective on things. He looked at his phone, and wondered who would be first to call. He got his answer as he was driving through Lee Green.

It was Amisha: 'H, it's me. Are you alright? I've just seen what happened.'

'Hello Ames. Yes, I'm fine, no need to worry about me. What have you seen?'

'Well, it's all over the place. On Twitter it's film and pictures of you being chased out of the Naismiths building by a baying mob, and being knocked to the ground. "Fascist *agent provocateur* chased out of Naismiths College", it says. They're gloating like you would not believe. Were you injured?'

'No, not a scratch on me. Despite Master Toby's best efforts. Who posted that?'

'You'll never find them H, it's an anonymous group account.'

'In what name?'

'Lewisham Antifa.'

H let out a heavy sigh; there was obviously still much to learn. 'Who, or what, is Antifa, Ames?'

'A group of middle class toytown revolutionaries. They dress up in black and act up a lot, but most of them still live with their mums. You seem to have poked a hornet's nest of them. What were you doing there?'

'Oh, just working a little case, nothing to write home about. A kid got bashed up by that lot, or someone like them, and one of the lecturers has had him slung out. She's running the place like an indoctrination camp in Chairman Mao's China. I'm working for the parents.'

'Interesting.... Let me guess – you thought it was going to be an amusing little walk in the park, money for old rope, yes?'

'Yep, something like that.'

'Well, these people may look like clowns, but some of them are capable of doing plenty of damage.'

'So I am coming to understand, Ames.'

'OK, well if there's anything I can do to help.'

'Funny you should say that. Fancy a bit of dinner tonight?'

***

He got off the phone with Amisha just as he pulled up outside his house. Olivia had never been much of a curtain-twitcher, but she was twitching them now. She came out front and intercepted him as he walked towards the house with a big hug.

'H, what the hell happened? I just saw...'

'It was nothing, babes. Don't worry, I've just been hanging about with some sociology students and their teacher, not going toe-to-toe with some Russian gangster bent on revenge. I had a tiny little run-in with them, and they've made it look like World War Three. It was nothing, really.'

'Well, how was it? I take it the students weren't very cooperative?'

'Imagine you were writing a story, or making a film or whatever, and you wanted to make them as pathetic and weird as you possibly could. Then double it.'

'You're exaggerating H.'

'Nope. And the teachers are worse. You should've seen the way their teacher's got them brainwashed. It's easy to see how they can be wound up like little toy soldiers and sent out to do all sorts.'

'Like attack statues of war heroes?'

'Exactly.'

Olivia gave H another peck on the cheek, and said 'Why don't you sit yourself down. I'll put the kettle on and we can talk.'

'I thought we might shoot down to Bluewater or somewhere – I need to do a bit of shopping.'

'Shopping? You? Have you have had a bump on the head?'

'Funny, Liv. Very funny. Why don't you just get the boy ready? If we leave now we can beat the traffic.'

'Alright babes,' said Olivia, disengaging herself from him and moving towards the front room, 'but what on earth is it you want to buy? Is there a new Sinatra box set out?'

'Nah, I need to get a few bits and pieces, for this case. I can't go back to Naismiths looking like Detective Inspector Harry Hawkins, dog lackey of the fascist state, can I?'

'You mean there's more to do? You're going back there, after what happened today?'

'Yep. The Phillipsons and their boy deserve justice – I'll tell you all about it in the car. Anyway, the leader of that little dog's dinner over there is a lecturer called Poppy Stackridge. She is an absolute horror, and I mean to sort her out. I'm bringing Amisha in to help me. I'm meeting her for dinner later, by the way.'

\*\*\*

H spent the next morning trying on his new wardrobe, talking to Justin, and scanning Olivia's social media – having none of his own – for reactions to his adventures of the previous day. These turned out to be exactly as he'd expected, and by mid-morning he'd switched off his phone in response to the constant stream of calls from friends and former colleagues queuing up to ridicule him.

In the afternoon he took Little Harry for a swings-and-roundabout session and kickabout in the park. This helped take his mind off the absurdities he was now embroiled in, and when he got home he backed it up by going deep into his film archive and picking out *Pimpernel Smith* with Leslie Howard, which always gave him a lift.

At five o'clock he drove to Amisha's place via Greenwich market, where he picked up a couple of small red lapel badges to complete his costume – one Che Guevara, one hammer-and-sickle. He and Amisha shared a bottle of wine – she was in high spirits, and did not appear to be taking the mission very seriously – and finalized the plan. Amisha would cover the Naismiths Tavern, the Orc and Goblin and the student union bar, while H would focus on the Marquis of Grimsby and be in general circulation. If they found themselves in the same place at the same time they were not to acknowledge one another, in case H was spotted and Amisha tainted by association. H was going in, at Justin's suggestion, as an old-school comrade trying to drum up interest in the Revolutionary Communist Party. Amisha, in a headscarf, would be distributing flyers and stickers for a fake upcoming 'Stop the City' demonstration.

They took a cab. H got out of it in Deptford and walked down to New Cross, while Amisha stayed in all the way to the college. The area was buzzing with Friday night energy. She entered the college and went to the student union bar. She ordered a barely-drinkable white wine and downed it in one, trying to keep it clear of the enamel on her teeth on its way down, pulled a handful of flyers from her bag and pinned them purposefully to noticeboards already overloaded with information about meetings, demonstrations, associations. One notice indicated that an 'informal' Boycott Israel meeting should already be underway on the premises. That looked promising, and she went in search of it; but the place was heaving with young drinkers, the air thick with their excited talk and loudly amplified hip-hop and dub music, and she could see nothing that looked as formal as even an informal meeting. She moved through the crowd and made herself as visible as possible by attaching stickers to walls, hoping someone would want to catch up with her and talk later, or at least send an email to the hotline address provided. The night was young. She left the building and headed for the Orc and Goblin, wondering how H was getting on across the road.

The big man himself had already hit the buffers in the Marquis of Grimsby, despite his best efforts at putting together a convincing incognito. The trouble started as soon as he'd surged in through the door and taken his first turn around the pub. Snowy Bedford was plotted up at the bar with his little firm.

*Oh fuck it, that's all I need.*

H looked like a half decent pseudo-revolutionary in battered leather jacket, hipster cap, sunglasses, faded jeans, Che Guevara badge and all. 'Fuck me H,' Snowy said as he approached, 'I didn't know it was fancy dress in here tonight. What've you come as, Poppy Stackridge's bitch?'

The wave of crazed drunken laughter that issued from Snowy's group in response to this was all it took. Heads turned, and H felt a couple of the students he'd seen in action the day before clock him from a corner table. He pulled his cap down further, and his collar up higher, but he knew the game was up.

'Thanks for absolutely fuck-all, Snow,' he said. 'I'll have a pint of Guinness and a Jamieson's. What gave me away?'

'Everything mate, the way you hold yourself, the way you walk, everything. Anyone who knows you could spot you a mile off. It'd take more than a comedy hat and an old leather jacket to disguise you, you soppy old bastard.'

157

'Yeah, I never was much good at all this undercover palaver. I tried it a couple of times at the met, and it didn't go well then either.'

'No, you were always more of a full-frontal man. Here I am, take me or leave me, weren't it? Anyway, sorry if I've fucked things up mate. What was it, sort of a fact-finding thing?'

'Yep, but it's not over yet, Snow. I've got someone else working with me. The plan was to put ourselves about and see if we can't root out a whistleblower, someone from the inside who'll tell us about what happened to the Phillipson kid. And I'll take anything I can get on this Poppy Stackridge. She needs taking down a peg or two.'

'I make you right, H. Fancy another pint?'

'Yeah, go on then. I'm not much use now they know I'm about. I'll stay here with you and your mates, in case I need back-up. I should think big Toby'll be on the hunt for me by now,' said H, suppressing a giggle.

\*\*\*

But Toby was not on the hunt for him; Toby was in the Orc and Goblin, drinking cider with Amisha. She'd spotted him as soon as she walked in – in truth, he was a hard boy to miss – and checked H's photo of him just to make sure before approaching him and coquettishly putting stickers on his upper arms and the front of his t-shirt.

Now they were deep in conversation about the evils of capitalism and the tightening screw of state fascism, the ills of the world in general, and Toby's very personal struggle with his own privileged background. He'd packed a good few ciders under his belt during the happy hour, and was now very much in confessional mode. Amisha listened with interest, and made mental notes as stories and details spilled carelessly out of him. She was having to wait a long time for pauses in his flow, but eventually she spotted an opportunity to get something useful out of him as he hit a peak of emotion on the theme of the duties of the revolutionary, and the ends justifying the means.

'So what are you saying, Toby? That men who will not willingly forego their privileges, men unlike yourself, should be made to do so by force?'

'Yes. Absolutely. Or nothing will ever change.'

'Change to what?'

'Er...to everyone being the same, to the end of tyranny.'

'Oh. Interesting,' said Amisha. 'So you advocate a hands-on approach to ending oppression?'

'I do. Totally.'

'Are you active on this front yourself?'

'Well, no names, if you know what I mean. But yes, I have been busy.'

'Good for you. How exciting. Can I get you another drink?'

Amisha went outside into the street and phoned H. He answered the call, sounding very merry and bright. 'Working hard, H?' she said.

'Well, no, if I'm honest. They tumbled me straight away in here, with a little bit of help from Snowy fucking Bedford. How you are getting on?'

'I've got a live one here; your friend Toby. He's drunk, and I've got him on the verge of spilling the beans. He wants to talk. I've almost got him. Another cider or two and he's going to give me the lot.'

'Blinding,' said H. 'Top girl. Listen Ames, take him into the pub garden, away from the music, and record him.'

'Would that stand up in court H, with him being drunk, and me leading him on? It's entrapment, no?'

'It might, or it might not. But it'll be worth having Ames, we can use it to put pressure on the college. And Stackridge. See if you can get him to mention any other names. If he

159

gets drunk enough, and gushy, bat your eyes at him and make him think he's got a chance, and straight-out ask him if it was him who hammered Martin Phillipson, or if not if he knows who did.'

'I'll get you your answers H, but I think I'll do it my way,' said Amisha.

***

H returned to the Phillipson's house on Monday morning, less than a week since his first visit, with good news for them. With the greetings done, and the tea made and produced, and everyone settled comfortably into the plush furniture, he gave it:

'Right, to summarise: after a full weekend's pressurizing my colleague and I have managed to collect two signed statements from people with knowledge of the events around your son's beating. Both are prepared, if it comes to it, to state in court that they heard Poppy Stackridge issue a direct instruction to a group of students to mask up, jump your son, confiscate the fez and administer the punishment beating. They independently collaborated her final call to action word for word: "No-one's pretending to be Tommy Cooper on my watch. Let's take this fascist bastard down".'

The Phillipsons listened with grave intensity; no whoops and hollers or triumphal punching of the air for them. 'Did either of these two participate in the attack?' said Mr. Phillipson.

'Not that they'll admit to. I think one of them probably did – namely one Toby Cholmondeley. But he's not going to hold his hands up for it. He's got too much to lose, with his posh family and all. He's going to leave the college, I think.'

'Why so?' said Mrs. Philipson.

'Well, it seems like he's had enough. He's been under a lot of pressure. He's got to be one of the most confused

160

individuals I've ever come across. Ashamed of his aristocratic background, ashamed of being a man, ashamed of being British, ashamed of everything he is...you name it. He's got the lot. Stackridge picked up on his youthful confusion and turbo-charged it, and told him the oppressors would just have to get a kicking. He even had a pop at me. Managed to put me on the floor. Anyway, I've straightened him out, over the weekend, or started to. These kids are being cleverly exploited, Mr. Phillipson – most of them are just too young and clueless to know any better.'

'Tell that to Martin,' said Mr. Phillipson. 'I never had you down as a bleeding heart, Mr Hawkins - not by a long chalk.'

'Dealing with this lot has opened my eyes. These kids basically crave a strong authority figure despite, or because of, years of not experiencing any and being told authority is bad. People like Stackridge know that, and just exploit the kid's earlier brainwashing. That's my assessment, anyway. It's the grown-ups who are the real problem.'

'Which brings us to the lecturess,' said Mrs. Phillipson.

'Yes. These two statements should be more than enough to get the ball rolling with a suit. And probably a criminal case, if your son can be persuaded to press charges. I would say you're in a very good position to get him reinstated in short order, and then sue the hind legs off them. Or get them to settle out of court.'

'It's not the money, Mr. Hawkins. It never was. I think, in the end, I wanted the point made about how easy it was for all this nonsense to take hold. War heroes who fought fascism desecrated, people prevented from speaking just because they have a different point of view. Do you agree, Mr Hawkins? Do you not hear the sound of Winston Churchill spinning in his grave, deep in the night?'

H, who'd come to Tonbridge more or less straight from an all-night reunion drink with Snowy Bedford and a few of the old Bermondsey boys, was too tired and hungover to

161

want to hear his own style of ranting reflected back at him, so he just said 'Oh, I hear it Mr. P. I hear it. All the bloody time.'

# Tipping Point

# Friday 18th January: 1974

'Well Hawkins, you've surpassed yourself this time,' said the Headmaster. 'What do you have to say for yourself?'

'Nothing, Sir.'

'Nothing. Nothing? I've got three boys badly injured, one in hospital having his nose re-set, parents wanting to press criminal charges against you, and chaos all over the school. Listen, it's like a baboon enclosure out there. And about all this you have nothing to say?'

'No Sir.'

'No, boy! No? You hit Gary Milton in the face with a fire extinguisher, correct?'

'Well, yes Sir, but…'

The Headmaster, his jaw working furiously, retrieved the cane leaning against the wall in the corner of the room and flexed it, his eyes fixed on the boy's.

'You exasperate me, Hawkins, you really do. You're a bright boy – lazy as hell, but bright – the best athlete in the school, the other boys in your year clearly look up to you, and yet you're here in my office time and again, for one thing or another. Fighting, insubordination. Well?'

'Well what, Sir?'

'Illuminate me boy, illuminate me. Normally I'd give you six strokes with this, as per usual,' the Headmaster said, lifting the cane, 'but you've had plenty of that medicine, to no effect as far as I can tell. I fear we're beyond all that now. I'm going to have to suspend you from the school at the very least, and in the end probably expel you. Speak to me, man-to-man…what is your problem?'

'Well, they were bullying Epimou again, Sir. The three of them, they're on him all the time, he's only little, he wouldn't hurt a fly. I wasn't having any more of it, I decided to put a stop to it.'

'By stamping on one boy's head and striking another full in the face with a fire extinguisher?'

'He came at me with a chisel, Sir. Milton – he had a chisel, from the woodwork room.'

The Headmaster sank heavily into his chair and fell silent. The boy, standing to attention on the other side of the desk, waited.

The clock ticked. The Headmaster sighed heavily, and maintained his silence. His eyes glazed over, and for a time he seemed to be far away. Sounds of boys running and shouting punctuated the silence.

Someone set off the fire alarm. The Headmaster stirred. 'Have you read Lord of the Flies, Hawkins?'

'No Sir, what's it about?'

'It's about you, boy – you and your friends. Read it. It looks like you're going to have plenty of time on your hands. Go home. Leave the premises immediately. I'll try to calm Milton's parents down, and I'll talk to the staff, and I'll phone your parents this afternoon with my final decision – tell them not to get their hopes up.'

The boy turned and headed towards the door.

'And Hawkins…'

'Yes Sir?' the boy said, wheeling around.

'One last piece of advice. The Army, get yourself into the Army. You have something in you, son – let the Army bring it out. Don't waste your time and energy hanging around with these louts. You'll be sixteen soon. Get yourself into the army.'

***

Harry took his time getting home. He lived only a short walk away from the school, on a council estate on Raymouth Road, but by the time he'd wandered along Southwark Park Road, lingering for a while around the stalls in the market, and made a tour of Southwark Park itself, it was dark. It was dark, and the streets were dirty, and it was wet, and he was cold.

He approached the flat, key in hand, wondering whether the lights would go out tonight and they would have to eat their dinner by candlelight again, while his dad ranted and raved about the 'unions holding the fucking country to ransom.'

His mum was waiting. There was no sign of his dad, or his two younger brothers, but his mum was waiting. The diminutive and elegantly dressed but highly-strung Eileen Hawkins – a harassed and exhausted looking figure at the best of times – was standing at the top of the stairs, arms folded, lips pursed, as he came through the door.

'Dynamite comes in small packages,' his dad always said when she blew up, or was on the verge of it, and Harry saw that she was on the verge of it now. He gulped hard and headed upward, watching his feet move up the stairs, as if they belonged to someone else, as he went.

'Kitchen. Now,' his mum said through clenched teeth. He followed her in.

\*\*\*

'Well?' she said.

'Well what?'

'Don't you "well what" me boy. Tell me something – do you ever think about me, about my nerves, before you do these stupid things?'

'Little' Harry – he was already almost six feet tall – looked at his feet and shuffled about for a bit and said nothing. The room fell silent, except for the grinding of Eileen Hawkins' teeth.

'Well,' the boy said at length, deciding not to let her rage grow in silence, 'there was a kid getting bullied, they were giving him a proper kicking, I couldn't just ignore it.'

'So you smashed someone's face in with a fire extinguisher and put him in hospital? Jesus Harry, what will your dad say?'

'He'll say I done the right thing.'

'About you being thrown out of school, you silly little bastard, I meant about you being thrown out of school.'

'He won't care. He wants me to leave anyway and start working.'

'And be like him? Getting up at four o'clock every day and working like a dog in all weathers. Harry, I wanted you to get an education, so you could do something with your life.'

'What's wrong with being a tipper driver? What's wrong with dad's life? He gets hold of a nice few quid, looks after us alright, doesn't he?'

Eileen Hawkins shook her head, collapsed into a chair, and sighed the sigh of ages. 'It's a waste of time talking to you now boy, you don't know enough. You'll understand one day I suppose, when you've all finished wearing me away and I'm in my grave.'

She reached for her purse and pulled out a five-pound note. 'Make yourself useful,' she said, 'go and get the fish and chips. And bring me the receipt.'

# Saturday

'Fucking hell mate, that's a touch. I wish they'd sling me out as well. I could get a job and start getting hold of some money. No cunt will lend me a penny now.'

John Viney – Shy Nervous John to his friends – hauled himself out of bed and pulled his trousers on. His mum had shown Harry into his room, and his friend had established himself on the floor, in the tiny space not strewn with chocolate wrappers, clothes, records, and piled-up copies of New Musical Express and Melody Maker.

'Yeah mate, it's well good to be out of it. I've told my mum and dad that's my lot. I'll start looking for a job Monday.'

'Sweet.'

'Yep, it certainly is. Come on mate, it's nearly eleven o'clock, there's a coat I want to look at in Lord John. Let's get up there,' said Harry.

'Alright mate, but I want to go to the HMV in Oxford Street as well, there's a new Faces album out. And Deep Purple. And I want to look at the imports, there's new Lou Reed and Steely Dan and Todd Rundgren albums coming out soon. I've got to get hold of some fucking money mate. I can't risk nicking them anymore, not after what happened the other week,' said John.

'What, you worried about that little security guard?'

'Yeah, he's bound to remember me. I did give him a clump as I was shaking him off.'

'More like a little slap really mate, weren't it?'

'It was more than a slap mate, he went down like a sack of shit, and you know it.'

'Yeah, alright Johnny Big Bollocks...sort yourself out. We haven't got all fucking day. I need to be back by six to get ready,' said H.

Saturday night at the Elephant and Castle. Harry, resplendent in his new black crushed-velvet jacket and purple flares, and John, in the soppy Afghan coat he insisted on wearing and that everyone took the piss out of, were out and about with a few of their mates. The Elephant was great; the Odeon would let practically anyone in to see the 18-certificate films. Tonight, it was Bruce Lee in *Enter the Dragon*, and after that The Pineapple, where they'd serve anyone who could do a decent impression of a seventeen-year-old — and it was wall-to-wall dolly birds. Harry had an established, well-oiled routine: a nice few pints, pull a little sort, knee-trembler round the back of the pub, in the shadow of the Draper House tower block. Nothing better.

They swarmed into the cacophonous pub at half-past nine, practicing their Kung Fu moves as they came. Harry went straight to the bar and got a round, and the boys plotted up by the little stage where the DJ was. The evening was building, beginning to move towards its climax. *Hi Ho Silver Lining* blared from the speakers. Harry surveyed the scene, and liked what he saw. It was basically a glorified youth club, except everyone was drunk and the fruit he was after was hanging very low on the trees.

One familiar looking blond girl caught his eye; she was small, and as provocatively mini-skirted and stack-heeled as the rest, but there was something about her. She was wearing less make-up than her friends, he could really see her face. She was looking him straight in the eye, smiling at him.

He squeezed his way through the heaving crowd and introduced himself.

'Hello darling, how are you tonight? I'm Harry.'

The girl laughed.

'What's so funny?'

'Harry…bit old fashioned ain't it?'

'Well, if you're going to…'

'No, I like it. It's a real man's name. I'm Julie. You don't remember me, do you?'

Again with the smile.

'Should I?'

'I think you should, yes. I talked to you last year when some girls from our school came on that visit to yours – you know, when they were showing us around. Maybe I look different.'

'Yeah, I should think you've come on nicely since then. Pleased to meet you Julie. Fancy a drink?'

'No, you're alright. I've had enough, thanks.'

'Dance, then?'

She raised her arms and let him take her, and he took her by the waist and moved her to the dancefloor.

\*\*\*

They danced – Brown Sugar, Drive-in Saturday, Metal Guru, Crocodile Rock – until Harry decided the time was right.

'Fuck me, is it hot enough in here? Fancy coming outside?'

'What for?' Julie said.

'You know, a breath of air, a little chat.'

'And?'

'And nothing. I like you. I thought we could just go outside for a bit.'

'A bit of what…a bit of knee-trembling round the back?'

'Well, I…'

'You're going to have to do better than that Harry. What do you think I am, one of these slags?' she said, gesturing to the room at large.

Harry was crestfallen, and embarrassed, and didn't know what to say. Or do. He was itching to get away. He relaxed his grip on her waist and made ready to go.

'I tell you what though,' the girl said before he could move, smiling warmly, her blue eyes glistening in the semi-darkness, making his head swim, 'you can take me out if you like. Somewhere nice, when you can afford it. I'm here every week.'

She gave him a peck on the cheek, squeezed his hand and left him to it.

He fought his way to the bar, alone, ordered a pint, gulped it down like a man who'd just crawled out of a desert, and ordered another. There were butterflies in his stomach, and he felt elated, as if he could float above the people around him and watch them from the ceiling. He didn't know how to name what he felt; but he knew what he was going to do.

# Sunday

He got up early, popped a couple of painkillers for his head and went for his run. His usual was a few laps of Southwark Park, a surge along the Blue, down to Tower Bridge Road and back again. He liked to be on the road for three quarters of an hour or so. He hadn't been to the gym for weeks, since he'd had a bollocking for being a lazy bastard from Billy Marshall the coach, but he kept up his road running because it made him feel better and he liked the feeling of being strong, and lean, and ready. Ready for what – beyond being able to defend himself against all comers on the street, as was necessary for a fifteen-year-old boy in Bermondsey – he didn't yet know.

He'd been boxing for school and club for a couple of years on and off, and had won a few bits and pieces. His dad, Marshall and a few others had told him he had the makings of a fighter, but his heart wasn't really in it anymore, and he was losing interest. His growing enthusiasm for girls, and beer, and going to the football were undermining his dedication. But he ran, and he worked out at home, and he felt ready like a fighter should, and he waited. He was nearly sixteen now, suddenly no longer a schoolboy, and about to start making his own way in the world, one way or another.

'Stay sharp son,' Marshall had told him, 'always stay sharp, you never know what's coming next.'

\*\*\*

On this particular Sunday morning what came next was a place at the table, fighting with his brothers and dad over their portions of a full English breakfast. He loved these Sunday breakfasts – the food, of course, the smell of fried fat hanging in the air; but he also loved the noise, the action, the quarrelsome energy of four males hungry for more bacon, sausage and fried bread. His mum always tried to establish order, his dad – a huge, larger than life and difficult to manage figure – always took things in the direction of chaos: encouraging the boys' confrontations, winding them up, roaring with laughter when they took his bait, and clipping them round the ear – for mum's benefit, Harry always thought, rather than his own – when they got out of hand.

'Enough! I've had enough!' shouted Eileen, 'Finish your breakfasts and get out of my kitchen, the lot of you!'

Harry's dad gave him the wink and said 'We better get out of here son, looks like she's on the warpath. I'm going downstairs for a quick sluice. Why don't you come for a light ale with me – I want to talk to you. I'll be ready in half an hour.'

***

They walked into the fugged-up pub at a quarter past twelve; it was just beginning to roar. They made their way to Big Harry's usual table and were greeted by the usual crew of Sunday lunchtime drinkers. Stevie Parker shouted 'Oi! Oi! Here they are…Harry H and the Boy Wonder. How are you son, how's your cock dangling? Been putting it about? I assume you've worked out where it is?'

'I can find it alright, don't you worry about that you fat old bastard, and put it about – when was the last time you or your old woman saw yours?' The company at the table – Parker himself, Heart-Attack Albert Perkins, Billy Pickett, Harry's uncle Arthur – burst into roaring approval; the boy was one of them now.

You had to give as good as you got. Harry had learned that on his first rite-of-passage trip to the pub with his dad at the age of 13. 'Give it back to them son,' his dad had told him on the way in, 'give it back to them. They'll give you

175

plenty of stick, so give it back to them. Always stand up for yourself, always...don't back down, or let anyone really take the piss out of you.'

By now Harry, at the age of fifteen, was a seasoned pubgoer and drinker who could hold his own against even the most demanding of his dad's mates.

'Come with me son,' Harry's dad said, motioning him towards the bar, 'I want to have a word with you before we get involved.'

They stationed themselves at the end of the heaving bar.

'What is it Pop?'

'I want you to come to work with me next week, starting tomorrow. I've got a lot on and I need an extra pair of hands or two. A fiver in your hand at the end of the day if you perform.'

'Doing what?'

'Well, you know what's going on with the government, and the unions, and the three-day week, and the wildcat strikes and all that?'

'Yeah, more or less. I've seen the news, and I've heard what you say about the "fucking miners" ...and I can't help noticing that the lights keep going out at night.'

'Alright boy, slow down, don't get clever. I need someone to help me load the tipper up, bags and boxes of rubbish mostly. The dustmen have been on strike for a fortnight in Kensington and Chelsea. There's rubbish and shit piling up everywhere, rats running about, you name it. The posh mob over there are screaming and the council want it all sorted out. Me and a few of the boys have arranged with them to get over there and tidy it all up, off the books. So I need hands. Might go on for a week or two. Fiver a day, if you graft. Plenty of readies in your pocket. Fancy it?'

Harry did the numbers in his head – twenty-five quid for a week's work. An unimaginable sum of money.

What the fuck must they be paying the old bastard?

'Yep, I'm in Pop, course I am.'

'Good man. One other thing, things might get a bit tasty over there. We're strike-breaking, so the dustmen and their soap-dodging union mates will have the hump. If they see us they'll try to stop us. You might have to put your boxing skills to use. OK?'

This was getting more interesting by the minute. Harry made his dad wait a few seconds.

'Alright Pop, I'll have it…if you stick a quid a day on top of the fiver. Danger money.'

Big Harry roared with laughter, patted his boy on the back, peeled a five pound note from his wad, told him to get the beers in, and turned to go back to the table.

'One other thing Pop,' said Harry. 'Do you need anyone else, or just me? Sounds like a lot of work.'

'Like who?'

'My mate John – he needs to get hold of some money.'

'John who?'

'John Viney – you know, Shy Nervous John.'

'That great long streak of piss? Are you having a laugh?'

'No, he'll be alright. He really needs the money.'

'Well, he strikes me as being a bit of a moocher. And I've seen more fat on a burnt fucking chip. Will he pull his weight? Can he look after himself?'

'Not really, but if there's any trouble he'll be away quicker than a rat up a drainpipe. He'll be the Invisible Man – you won't have to part with any danger money for him.'

The old man mulled it over.

'Alright, let him come tomorrow and I'll have a look at him. He can have three quid. Tell him to meet us at half four.'

'In the morning?'

'Yes, in the morning. What do you think this is, a fucking holiday camp?'

177

# Monday

Harry had never been so cold in his life; he'd had no idea such cold existed. He was not wearing a hat, as he'd been advised to do, and his ears were hurting so much he wanted to cry. His whole body was shaking. He could scarcely believe his dad did this every day, day in, day out, starting early, working till dusk, barrelling around London carrying hardcore, rubble, sand, dirt – whatever had to be moved around whenever buildings were being destroyed or getting built.

They were sitting in the cab of his dad's tipper, trying to get some warmth out of the tiny heater and surveying the shattered-looking yard in the early gloom – parked-up tippers, piles of tyres and assorted motor parts, a dimly lit Portakabin in which other freezing men were brewing up their first teas of the day. Overhead the early trains thundered deafeningly into London Bridge, and in the gaps in between them the traffic could be heard, but not seen, building up on Ilderton Road.

Shy Nervous John turned the corner of a massive, blackened railway arch and shuffled into view, hunched and shivering and bent forward into the cold, at four thirty-five. Harry's dad started the engine and roared 'Come on son, we haven't got all fucking day,' motioning to the approaching boy to get a move on. John broke into a trot, came alongside the passenger door and Harry hauled him up.

They moved out at a crawl – the government had imposed a twenty-miles per hour speed limit to save fuel – onto Ilderton Road, along the Old Kent Road as far as the Elephant and Castle, left through Kennington, right at the Oval tube and across Vauxhall Bridge. All at twenty miles per hour, Harry's dad cursing to himself the whole way about the state of the country and the useless Prime Minister,

'Ted fucking Heath', before snapping out of it with 'Right boys, all set? Easy money today, it's growing on trees over there. Heave them bags up, keep your wits about you, do as you're told and we'll all be laughing, and going home caked-up with readies. How does that sound?'

Harry and John smiled and felt good – they were warmer now, the sun was up, big money was coming their way, and they didn't have a care in the world.

\*\*\*

They noticed it as soon as they crossed the border of Westminster and got into Kensington and Chelsea, and by the time they reached Victoria Station they could hardly believe what they were seeing – piles, mounds, mountains of rubbish bags and boxes and other assorted filth on the pavements, spilling into the road in places so that the traffic had to skirt round it, all of it stinking to high heaven.

Harry's dad took his hands off the steering wheel as they cruised past the station, rubbed his hands together and laughed out loud. 'Lovely jubbly. We are fucking quids-in here boys! Have a look at this lot, they'll need us here for weeks sorting all this out. God bless the strikers!'

Harry laughed with him, for it seemed to him that they had indeed entered the land of milk and honey. Six quid a day, every day, for weeks or more – just for heaving rubbish onto the back of the tipper. He saw visions of shopping excursions into the West End for clothes, presents for and dinners with Julie, big nights out on the beer with the boys. Getting slung out of school was the best thing that had ever happened to him. Now he was beginning to live!

They turned into a street the like of which Harry had never seen before, except on the television – huge, imposing white-fronted houses, with very expensive cars parked up outside them. Harry had more Rolls Royces and Bentleys in his field of vision than he'd ever seen in his life. And all around the cars the rubbish, everywhere along the iron railings in front of the houses, spilling out of its boxes and bags, teeming with rats. But even in its current state he could see that this was as posh as it got; it reminded him of *Upstairs Downstairs*, which his mum watched religiously on Sunday evenings. He supposed that he and his little firm would be working downstairs today.

'No wonder this mob round here have got the hump, Pop – how much are these houses worth?'

'More than you'll ever see son. Let's get cracking. It's a quarter to six now, we've got to fill the back up and get down to Deptford to tip it. I've got a bloke I know in one of the council dumps straightened out. Even at twenty miles an hour we can do seven or eight loads a day. I hope your mum made you some sandwiches John.'

John nodded and smiled, weakly.

'Here, put these on boys,' said Harry's dad, throwing each of them a pair of thick gardening gloves. 'On we go, do your duty, keep your wits about you, give me a shout if you see anyone you don't like the look of lurking about.'

*\*\*\**

'Fuck this for a game of soldiers,' said John, ignoring the boxes and picking gingerly through the bags, looking for ones that weren't split, terrified of the rats, sick to his stomach.

'Shut it John, the old man'll go potty if he hears you moaning. Just get on with it. Think of the readies.'

Harry and his dad – who was at the other end of the street, working his way down towards them – had been lifting, heaving bags and running back and forth to the tipper for an hour, grafting like demons. The morning was gloomy, a light but freezing drizzle had set in, and it was dirty and

180

unpleasant work, having to scoop up and carry not only bags and boxes but often the exposed, stinking household refuse that the rats had exposed.

John was clearly out of his depth among the filth, and the backbreaking work, and the threat of danger, and Harry had been covering for him. So far his dad had seemed oblivious, but Harry knew it was only a matter of time before he saw what was going on.

'Stay behind me John, just look busy as you can. Best thing you can do is keep look-out, I think the old man's expecting trouble.'

He didn't have to wait long. At eight o'clock, with the lorry two-thirds full, three men came barrelling into the street, screaming, shouting, gesticulating wildly. 'Get out of here you fucking scabs!' 'Get back in your motor and fuck off, you fucking scum!'

Harry's dad was on his way back from the tipper and towards another mound of rubbish when they appeared. He did not alter his pace; but only changed direction and headed towards the strikers. He was fifty yards or so from Harry and John, with the three men closing in on him fast.

Harry straightened up and ran towards his dad. By the time he arrived the first man was down, moaning and holding what looked like a broken jaw – Harry had never seen so crisp and decisive an uppercut in his life, and he felt a surge of pride and love for his father. The second man was throwing aimless and easy-to-dodge punches at a bobbing and weaving target, and the third had his arms around his dad's waist, trying to drag him down rugby style. Harry pulled the man off, wrestled him up straight and butted him full on the bridge of the nose; it cracked like a chicken bone, and a flood of crimson cascaded onto Harry's gloved hands.

'Touch my dad? Touch my fucking dad! I'll fucking kill you, you no-good cunt!'

Harry had lost control; he was screaming, and kicking at the prone man, and about to do much worse damage when he felt the vice-like grip of his father's arms around him, pulling him away. He noticed in his peripheral vision that the third man was also down, and not looking a lot better than the other two.

'Easy tiger, easy. That's enough, they've had all the treatment they need for today. Let's finish loading up – fuck knows how long it's going to take us to get to Deptford and back. Time is money, boy, time is money.'

# Tuesday

Harry's dad knew there'd be payback in Belgravia for Monday's shenanigans, and it was a very different looking outfit crammed into the tipper that pulled out of the yard at four thirty the next morning. Shy Nervous John was out – way out. No room for lightweights or fainthearts on the firm today. Harry was in though, along with two of his dad's mates – seasoned old-school growlers Terry Ruddock and Billy 'Tiny' Abbott, all 22 stone of him – who were in it as much for the promise of the fun and games as the money. Anyone who wanted to have a go at this little firm would have to come more than three-handed, and would have to know what they were doing.

But it had been a good day on Monday – they'd got five loads done in the end. Harry's dad was very happy with the day's takings, he was getting thirty quid a load, and the boy wonder himself had got a bonus.

They pulled into Eaton Place a little before five thirty and got straight down to it. Lifting, heaving, laughing, joking, making enough noise to wake the dead. Harry loved it, working in the early morning gloom alongside these characters, watching them, listening to them, learning the ropes. They filled the tipper up in less than half an hour and were about to jump up into the cab when the welcome committee arrived: eight burly dustmen, swarming at speed into the street, screaming blue murder.

'I tell you what H,' Terry Ruddock said, turning to Harry's dad, 'you're a man of your word, I'll give you that. You said it'd be lively over here today, and here's these boys come to say hello and we ain't even had our fucking breakfast yet.'

Harry gulped hard, and felt his guts start to wobble.

'Stand your ground son,' his dad said, 'nothing here we can't handle. Do the honours, will you Tine?'

183

Tiny Abbott jumped up into the cab surprisingly quickly for a man of his size, fished out four pick handles from behind the driver's seat, and was back in a flash, doling them out. Harry gripped his tight, feeling reassured by the heft and length of it.

'Anyone gets close enough to you, wrap that round his fucking nut for him. Stay behind us three if you can, but if it comes on top, let them have it. They're more scared of you than you are of them, they're only dustmen – go in hard and fast. He who hesitates is lost.'

The dustmen came on – slowly at first – with their 'Scabs!' and 'Traitors!' and the rest, but picked up the pace fifty yards out, slowing down again only when they got within ten feet of their target, suddenly looking unsure of themselves. Tiny Abbott smelled their fear and took it as his signal to run amok, wading into the strikers, using his pick handle like a scythe against the legs of the men in the vanguard, hammering into shins and knees and scattering the front rank like ninepins.

Four, five men in the rear jumped over their fallen comrades and surged towards Harry's firm, full of righteous anger. Not that it did them much good; Harry's dad and Terry Ruddock were all business. They moved straight towards the incomers, swinging their huge wooden staves like baseball batters, aiming at ribs, shoulders and occasionally heads. Harry stepped up himself for a piece of the action, and lost control again when one of the dustmen smashed a fulsome right-hander into his dad's face. Consumed by the need to avenge this, and flooded with adrenalin, he went after the culprit like a man possessed, clubbing him to the ground and kicking him in the ribs as hard as he could once the man was down.

He was running on feral energy, supercharged on the thrill of violence and barely reacting to the sirens that were coming closer and closer. He perceived the sound of them but didn't register their meaning until his dad pulled him away from the fray, dragging him backwards onto the pavement.

'That's enough son. Time for you to do the off. Get yourself home, walk away now. Tell your mother what's happened. Go, now...run!'

'But Pop...'

'Do as you are fucking told boy, get running, don't turn back.'

Harry did as was told. He set off running, back towards Belgrave Place, with his back to the melee. He heard the fighting being brought under control, the barked commands of the policemen, more sirens converging on the space he was rapidly leaving behind. Before he turned out of the street, by a small crowd of onlookers, he wheeled around, stopped and saw his father being forced to the ground by three policemen, who were applying their truncheons to his head with brutal precision.

He stood on the spot unable to move – unable to move forward to help his dad or backward to resume his retreat. He jogged on the spot, gasping for breath, tears stinging his eyes, in the grip of powerful emotions he'd never felt before. A meat wagon arrived and his dad, Terry Ruddock and Tiny Abbott, who was proving to be a handful for the half a dozen policemen swarming around him, were bundled into the back of it, along with three of the dustmen. The rest of their party were still on the ground, awaiting medical attention. An ambulance arrived. The meat wagon pulled away. Harry stopped moving; he stood still, steadied his breathing and waited until his reeling senses settled to the point where he could think what to do next.

His dad had told him to go home. He walked calmly, through rubbish-strewn, stinking streets, to Victoria Station, and without thinking, or paying, boarded a train to South Bermondsey.

185

# Wednesday

He awoke in the early afternoon, at one-thirty. His head was throbbing, and he began to recall the events of the previous afternoon and evening. He'd arrived home at lunchtime and given his mum the news. This was not the first time his dad had been taken into police custody, and she knew the drill. She made the phone calls, found out where he was and headed for Belgravia station, leaving Harry to hold the fort and keep an eye on his brothers.

He'd become tired and listless in the afternoon, and went hard at his dad's bottle of Southern Comfort, while the boys ran riot. When he'd taken care of that he found a bottle of scotch and gave that a hammering as well. He crashed out on his bed and only came-to later, when it was dark, when his mum got back and told him that his dad was still banged up and would be up before the beak in the morning.

It was still not two o'clock in the afternoon when he clambered out of bed, but the underwater murk of the January sky made it seem much later. He staggered to the bathroom and emptied the contents of his stomach, such as they were, and staggered back to bed. He turned the radio on, suffered through the news bulletin's usual litany of 'three-day week' – 'fuel shortages' – 'wildcat strike' – 'swarming rats' – 'government close to collapse' – 'crisis meeting'...and was rewarded with the O'Jays *Love Train*, a tune that always made him feel better.

He drifted off again, and when he came to it was dark, and the house was quiet, and there was a strange, stirring sort of song called *Cypress Avenue*. The DJ said it was Van Morrison. It wasn't his cup of tea, and it made him feel weird and restless, but something about it gripped him – something about a man describing his passion for a girl in a way Harry hadn't heard before, mainly because he seldom listened to the night time rock shows, unless he was at John's.

He sat up in bed after the song finished, and played the events of the previous day through in his mind, time and time again. He was feeling a mixture of feelings he found hard to put together, that wouldn't settle into any sort of pattern; rage, at the fact that someone was keeping his dad under lock and key; exhilaration, at the role he'd played in the drama; concern, for the man he'd clubbed to the ground with a pick handle – a man probably not that different from his dad, a man just trying to provide for his family; confusion, about why it had all happened, and what it all meant; guilt, for treating this beautiful girl Julie like a slag.

Less than a week ago he'd been a schoolboy. Now they were telling him he was a man, and was capable of doing things like a man. He tried to think about his future. There was no going back to school – that would just be a waste of time. Would he have to keep on with his dad, learning to drive the tipper and getting up at half past four every morning, ducking and diving and outsmarting and taking on all comers who tried to stop him looking after number one? Was that it? What else could he do, with no education or qualifications, and no real idea of what was out there for him?

He drifted off again.

***

He was awoken by the door slamming, and the voices of his mum and dad coming up the stairs, laughing and joking.

'Where are you son?' he heard his dad roar, 'I'm back, come to the kitchen and have a drink with me.'

Harry's parents were at the kitchen table, looking amused, when Harry joined them.

'What's happened to my scotch, you greedy little bastard...and my Southern Comfort? Fuck me, you must have been thirsty. This is all coming out of your wages, don't you worry about that,' his dad said, through an ear-to-ear grin.

'Anyway, how are you boy? Enjoy yourself yesterday?'

'Yeah...it was alright. How are you, what's happening?'

'It's all over son, all over. The council have smoothed it all over. No charges. They want it all kept quiet, they don't want the *Upstairs Downstairs* mob to know there's been a war on their streets, and if it gets out that they've been paying the likes of us to break the strike for them...not good. They've straightened Old Bill out, and we are all free men, my son, free men. Mind you, the job's over. It's back to the rubble tomorrow, big job just starting up in Camberwell. Nice few quid in it. You can have a lay in – I'll wake you up at half five.'

It was all Harry could do to hold back the tears welling up in his eyes, to bite his tongue and keep his unmanageable thoughts, and feelings, and confusion to himself. He was so happy to see his dad; so depressed at the thought of endless years of ducking and diving, of eating or being eaten, of having to make everything up as he went along. He loved his dad, loved his dad completely, hero-worshipped him, but did he want to be like him, really be like him?'

'Alright Pop,' he said, 'half five it is. You got a warm hat I can borrow?'

# Thursday

He set his alarm for quarter to five, and crept down the stairs and out of the house while it was still dark. It was still a long while to nine o'clock, but a good long walk would give him time to think things through, decide once and for all if he was doing the right thing.

It was freezing cold, and he pulled his dad's woolly hat down tight over his head as he set off towards Southwark Park Road. He would go up to Blackfriars Bridge, across the river, up into Fleet Street and along the Strand, and then into the West End.

Half-thoughts and images passed through his mind as he walked. He saw his dad, standing tall and fearless in the middle of a street fight, never taking a backward step, in this or anything else he did. His mum, tired, weary and worried about everything all the time, but happy and smiling as she came home from the police station with the man she loved. Julie, who'd looked at him with such shining eyes, her arms around his neck as they danced. John, shitting himself when things turned nasty, wanting nothing more than to just be left alone with his records and music papers. Stylianos Epimou, a good, harmless little kid constantly terrorised by thuggish morons like Gary Milton. Milton himself, lying on the ground with his nose in bits, crying like a baby. And the striking dustmen of Kensington and Chelsea, stretched out on the ground in helpless agony while his dad's utterly ruthless mates laid into them with wooden staves.

He crossed Blackfriars Bridge in bright, early morning sunshine and swung a left. It was eight o'clock by the time he got to Trafalgar Square, so he went for a slow turn around a tranquil and deserted St. James' Park, with its lake, its ducks, its nooks and crannies, its views of the Mall and Buckingham

Palace, and thought it was the most beautiful place he'd ever seen.

He coasted across the Mall and into Waterloo Place, and then up into Regent Street, feeling better than he had for a long time, maybe ever. He was calm, excited about the future, full of strength and energy. He was ready, ready for what came next. And so it was in a quietly exhilarated state that he moved, in measured, confident strides, across Oxford Circus and into Upper Regent Street.

It was nine o'clock on the dot, and the Army recruitment centre was just opening its doors. He was the first customer of the day, and the recruiting Sergeant at the desk seemed happy to see him.

'Good morning young man,' he said, 'and what can we do for you this fine morning?'

'Am I in the right place, for signing up?'

'Indeed you are, son, indeed you are. What exactly's on your mind?'

'Well...signing up – I want to sign up. I'm sixteen next week. I want to be a Paratrooper.'

###

# Did You Enjoy this Book?

Thank you for reading our book. If you enjoyed it, won't you please consider leaving us a short review. At your favourite online retailer Reader reviews are extremely important for independent authors.

Thanks!

Garry and Roy Robson

# About London Large

We've reached the end of our tour through some of the stories that feature H and other characters in the London Large series, and hope you enjoyed reading these shorts as much as we enjoyed writing them.

If you would like to get in touch with us we'd love to hear from you on anything in the above, on any of our novels or anything else you'd like to discuss. We reply to all emails. Our email address is: Garryandroyrobson@gmail.com

If you are a member we would be delighted if you support us on BookBub (bookbub.com) by selecting either or both of Garry or Roy as one of your favourite authors. They will automatically send you details of our new releases and it really helps us access additional BookBub promotional opportunities.

To say thank you we'd like to invite you to join our exclusive London Large readers club and offer you some of our work for FREE. All members of our club have access to free books and receive regular short stories before they become available elsewhere.
You'll also get news of all future releases at bargain prices. Joining is free, leave at any time.
To join just visit www.Londonlarge.com

## Novels in the London Large Series

*Blood on the Streets*
*Bound by Blood*
*Bloody Liberties*

*******

Printed in Great Britain
by Amazon

66154951R00111